A Run of a River

Rick Collins

Rick Collins

DEDICATION

To all the people carrying the pain of sexual abuse.
Your voices will be heard.

Rick Collins

CONTENTS

Rick Collins

ACKNOWLEDGMENTS

I want to thank Vangella Buchanan of The Writery Ink, LLC for her tireless work and support on all of my books. I also want to thank my wife Betsy and my children, Hannah and Sam, for all of their love and encouragement. I am because we are.

Rick Collins

Chapter 1

Rope Swing

Ken Richardson felt his lungs and the rest of his body working in unison, doing what it needed to be doing. He ran steadfastly along a narrow dirt path, in sight of the Merrimack River at the border of Beaumont and Tewksbury. His usual course took him up a steep hill and eventually within yards of the gardens that surrounded the dilapidated seminary where solitary men prepared themselves for the priesthood. There was a long stretch where his path was hidden by an open field, overgrown with weeds and struggling saplings. This was the part of his run where if he wanted it to be a good run, it would have to be painful.

He accelerated and strained against the rising heat. Some of the overgrowth slapped against his legs as he churned relentlessly toward the end of this particular, final run. Fields and forests work that way. They want to spread out and take over clearings that had yet to be subjugated. He wished that this part of his run, at this place and this very spot in Beaumont, could be kept from disappearing, but as his legs roiled and his arms pumped and his lungs strained for air, he realized that keeping this path clear was no longer his concern. Perhaps, someday, a runner might stumble upon this hidden path and make it usable again. A good path is a terrible thing to waste.

He ran on, effectively exhausted until finally, he came to the steepest hill on the trail, oily with moss and punctuated with gripping roots and biting rocks. He assaulted the hill nonetheless, grabbing roots and rocks to haul himself up to the summit where his run would come to its planned conclusion. He slipped once or twice, but the veins of the trees and the bones of the rocks formed a secure ladder and they held firm. With a final surge, on his hands and knees now, he climbed up and onto level ground. He righted himself, pulling in air from the clean of the summit. He brushed off some of the clinging dirt and muck of the hill and gross infestations from the fields. He stood there, done with his run, the overseer of the mighty Merrimack River.

He grew up not far from here, in a perfect neighborhood with completed landscaping and Friday evening gatherings. Children played tag or street hockey or baseball between the houses, thumping daring line-drives destined for backyard windows. Fathers drove woodies to work and mothers cleaned homes and fed children and drank together furtively on back porches. It was a quick bike ride to the forest from his house, fallen leaves marking hiking trails that led to the terminus of all paths, overlooking the Merrimack, lousy with dead fish. Ken thought back on it now and found it altogether ironic. That which began comes to its end here, not far from the fateful trail and covert crater. The forest was sacred to his friends, his family, his town. But hallowed wood can only conceal so much, not, at least, a truth hidden by rotting leaves, by the root ball of an upturned oak.

Of course, he hoped to be missed. No one leaves without

that desire. He walked a few yards and stepped close to the edge of the hill that dominated this part of his trail. He looked down one hundred feet to see the dam where the fish brook coursed through a water-treatment plant, long since failing at its purpose. The sun shined against the murk of the river and the conclusion of the brook and the rudeness of the concrete dam. He had fished in the place where the dam held back the brook to make a pond, small enough to swim across and deep enough to conceal old cars abandoned and rusted bikes discarded.

He glanced to his right and saw the old rope hanging from the second tallest oak, the one the neighborhood kids would use to swing out over the depthless pond or even over the unyielding dam. If you angled the rope properly, you had only the deep water to worry you, but if you adjusted the angle and ran at the rope differently, you could swing high above the dam and even out over the Merrimack. The bravest boys and girls chose that way, and the kids in the neighborhood cheered madly when someone made it out and back, grabbed onto by compatriots in horrified pleasure.

Ken pulled off the backpack he always wore when he ran. He took out an aluminum water bottle, still hard with ice cubes, and drank until the water was emptied. He wiped off the extraneous moisture from his mouth with his dirty hands and screwed back the top, misjudging the threads until he was finally able to find the right positioning to screw it back on properly. For some reason, this act of replacing the top to the water bottle rattled him. Why should it matter now that his water bottle had to be secured properly? He managed to get it right before he tossed the bottle to the ground.

Next, he changed out of his sweat-stained, dirty running clothes. He used his toe to take off one sneaker and then the next, not bothering to untie them, and left them to sit on the bank near the rope swing. He dug deeper into his backpack and pulled out a pair of gold, high-cut basketball shoes, the pair he had worn when he was just a kid. He took his balled-up running socks and his running outfit and tied them up with the laces of his old hoop shoes. He discarded the backpack and his running shoes on the trail. Walking naked before his God, he stepped quietly away from the second tallest oak with its dangling rope swing and approached the largest oak some fifty feet away, overturned many years ago, leaving a ball of roots and a dark hole where the tree had lost its hold, giving way during a terrible storm long forgotten.

He stood near the overturned tree, inhaling the richness of the soil and the contrasting rotted leaves. The sun was high in the sky now, casting no shadow over the ball of roots and cavernous hole. He took two steps closer, able now to see into the bottom where the dead roots still managed to hold onto their false claim to the earth. Running near here had always been a strain, but he did it daily, his self-flagellation now coming to an end. Some dark things can never heal. He looked deep into the hole and tossed in his tied-up clothes and his old basketball shoes, making sure they settled to the bottom of that cruel spot.

Ken jogged back to the rope swing. It was uncomfortable with his man parts bounding along, but a man goes out the way he comes in. Ken thought it ironic that this part of him was so exposed, always a source of shame and disgust, now

4

mattering not at all.

He dug into his backpack again and pulled out his new smartphone. His old one was already deep in the Merrimack. There would only be one video for people to scrutinize. Only one thing to share now. "It will hurt them when they unravel this," he thought to himself. He owed the town and the others that much, although he wasn't sure they would feel the same way. He turned on the video app and began to speak a long-rehearsed monologue. He didn't want it to last long.

"Some things are better left unsaid, so I'll keep it that way. Today was too much. I knew it would be too much. I've carried this long enough. It's time. Tell my friends that I wish I had been strong enough. I'm ok now with not being strong enough. Whoever really is?"

He adjusted the zoom of the smartphone camera to make sure the river and the pond and the dam were in view. Ken stooped down, bare ass almost touching the path, and set the camera against a small rock, perfectly positioned. He had tested the microphone to the new smartphone earlier in the day. He was sure the audio and video would be clear. That was important, he thought. Better no one misses anything. An unsparing act.

Ken turned on the record button and, taking hold of the rope swing, ran back a good twenty feet and then raced forward, driving his foot off the edge of the steep hill. His body arched gracefully over the middle of the pond. He thought he could make out a glint from one of the cars unknown people had hidden deep at the bottom. He swung back easily, the limb of the oak straining a little with a gentle sigh. He alighted gracefully on the ground not far from the phone and his first take-off spot. He let go of the rope and squatted down to make sure the recording was true. It was, and he knew it was a form of retribution that would cause pain, some sense of guilt and shame for some, perhaps as much as he had carried for so long. He put the phone back down against the rock, angling it slightly to the left, now turned away from the center of the pond and out toward the unhurried river. He checked to make sure he was alone. He found himself to be solitary amidst the watchful trees and the dusty running paths. To achieve the desired effect, his plan had to play out the way he intended.

He took hold of the rope again, this time walking back an extra ten feet. He knew from experience he would need more of a run-up to be successful. He took one more deep breath, holding on to the smells of this path and the soil and the forest and the pond and the river, holding on to them forever and perhaps to nothingness.

He was sure he would not be forgiven for what he was about to do. He was brought up understanding the depth of shame and completeness of guilt. Even at ten, he had already been taught that he was expected to clear his soul of its blackness, because of course, a little boy's soul was already corrupted by the soil of the world. The notion of it had been driven into him, nails through hands, by his parents and the Catholic school he attended, the myriad priests and nuns who molded his essence, his town and his neighborhood where children were brought to heel by parents of a greater generation, a constant reminder that he was bad and needed to atone for his impurities. So he would dutifully kneel at the altar after confession, made to pray for hours, *Holy, Mary, mother of God, pray for us sinners, now and at the hour of our death,* his knees bloody and his mind existentially hardwired to guilt and shame. His hell on earth was properly cultivated, and now he wondered what his next eternal fire would be like.

He glanced to his left, back toward the upturned oak. There was a new calmness for him now that the decision had been made as he thought about the oak and the hole and what he had just hidden there and what had always been hidden in its depths. Finally, breathing deeply once more, he grabbed the rope tightly and raced toward the cliff, launching himself. The rope and the bow of the oak complained loudly this time. His body swung out as far as it had ever done when he was a boy. He did not look down, instead, he used his instincts at the right time to make a final, athletic judgement. He was momentarily weightless, free at last, the arc of his swing reaching its apex. He felt the air above the Merrimack rush against his naked body. He no longer needed his grip. It was the perfect moment to do what he felt had to be done. He kept his eyes open for the duration of his descent. Some people believe it's not the fall that kills you; it's the sudden stop at the end. Ken Richardson had long understood the opposite to be true.

"Ken and Hank, ask your parents if you two would like to go to the Celtics game tonight. I have two extra tickets. They play the Lakers. Magic Johnson! We'll have a great time." Coach Jack.

Chapter 2

A Hometown Hero

The parade meandered through the streets of downtown Beaumont, with its fine bakeries and sandwich shops, restaurants and grocery stores, women's fashion boutiques and sporting goods shops, and banks with their facades of faux stone. Just before the road crested the hill to the academy, the parade swung left toward the old, run-down middle school with swampy baseball diamonds and a muddy football field.

Mayor Mickey Cummings rode in the first car. He held a long, bony cigar in one hand and waved to his townsfolk with the other. He had been mayor for ten years and had quite nicely stroked the comfort of his position, with few people willing or able to take him on in an election. Mayor Cummings squinted in the early morning sunlight. He continued to smile, occasionally putting the cigar to his mouth, inhaling deeply and letting out a long, thin wire of blue smoke. He held the cigar tightly with his jaws. It helped him present the facade of a benevolent leader, unencumbered with issues or concerns, only the cares of his constituents to distract him. This was a big day for the town, and whatever anger he felt within his being, he held onto it tightly as his teeth bit down on the rancid cigar. Better to conceal what he knew and keep the town alive. Everything was better that way. Hold it compressed within, the hate and loathing and fear of the truth of this day. It was what had been extorted from him, the price of his power. He tried not to buckle under the strain, convincing himself that it was for the good of the town. Lost souls sacrificed along the way, needful, it seemed, at the time.

Other dignitaries rode in convertibles that snaked along towards the playing fields and the celebration. They were preceded by the high school and junior high school marching bands, high stepping in unison, town fire-engines, polished red to perfection, police cars, red and blue lights strobing at epileptic intensity, boy and girl scout troops marching in militaristic precision, and rank upon rank of youth sports teams and their coaches, resplendent with the latest, most expensive gear. No expense was too small for the children worshipped by the parents of Beaumont. The happiness of the child was paramount, regardless of the reality of what it might do to them. Never disappoint beautiful Brie or handsome Johnny. It simply could not be done. They were worth the money, all of them, every penny of it.

The cookout started at ten in the morning. Thousands of townies ate from the long tables of donated lasagna dishes and mini hot dogs, salads, and cookies baked by the town cheerleaders, and yards and yards of burgers and sausage of every style. The aroma drew more and more people to the celebration, the crowd swelling into the thousands.

The two honorees were ushered up to the old bandstand where tables and chairs had been set for close family and town leaders. There was a microphone set up on a dais that stood some fifteen feet above the throng, better to get a good look at the honorees on this day, these very best from this quiet, quaint town.

Mayor Cummings took his seat just behind and to the right of the podium. Blue and gold balloons floated, attached by thin white string. Each string was long enough so the balloons would not bop the heads of the mayor when it came his turn to present the home-town heroes. Maybe it would have been better if the balloons drifted in front of him during his speeches, better to distract the townsfolk from the hideousness of the event and hide him from their stares. If only they knew just how dreadful the secret Mickey Cummings forced himself to bury.

Bernadette Thompson had been a long-time librarian in town. She had worked tirelessly to enhance the circulation that now was the envy of the state. Her grown children were there as was her husband, adorned in an old blue suit and a straw hat with a blue and gold band. Mickey got up and presented Bernadette to the town, shaking her hand first and then moving closer to give her a warm hug. He took out a velvet blue box and presented her with the key to the town, hanging from a blue and gold ribbon. He placed it around her neck and pecked her cheek lightly. She was overwhelmed with the adulation of the crowd and spoke of her enduring commitment to its readers, young and old alike. She sat down and cried for the rest of the celebration.

The second home-town hero was Jack Monroe. He was a fattening, balding man of about sixty who had tirelessly devoted most of his free time to the little boys of Beaumont. He was a legendary youth sports coach. The town had been split into two baseball leagues, American and National, separated by the railroad track that divided the town down the middle. His team was always the Red Sox. They had won countless town championships and he had been selected as the manager of the American League all-stars on numerous occasions. He worked at Bobby B's auto shop, one town over in Lawrence, fixing transmissions and repairing brake lines. His income was steady. He had no wife and kids, so he was free with his money, chaperoning countless trips for his baseball teams to Williamsport each summer for the Little League World Series. He paid for most of the trip for the fifteen boys on his team. He also put together all-star basketball teams that traveled Cape Cod, entering tournaments or playing against local towns like Barnstable and Falmouth, Orleans and Chatham, and even out on the islands.

For years, his teams played on Nantucket against the hardscrabble islanders who still fished for swordfish or halibut or cod or bluefin, sometimes a thousand miles off the coast. His hair was almost gone. He wore thick glasses that he always kept tight to the bridge of his nose by an elastic band that he fashioned around his head. His shirts tended toward plaid. Sometimes people joked that he could afford a different, more expensive style of clothing if he hadn't spent so much money on the kids in town. His slacks were perpetually khakis, cuffed always at the ankles, perhaps a bit too far off the ground, and he wore black and white Converse All-Star basketball shoes, whether it was at the service station or on the basketball courts or the baseball diamonds scattered around town. He would wear his basketball shoes until they ripped so hideously that he was shamed by the boys on his teams into buying himself a new pair. He never wanted to disappoint his boys.

Today was his day to stand before the town, receive its key, and join the ranks of hometown heroes. His name would be etched on a plaque at the town offices, where mayor Mickey Cummings held sway and blew large, sapphire rings of smoke from his cheap cigars while he did the town's business, usually with his feet up on his desk. This was Jack's day, and he basked in the warmth and love of the town. After a long speech given by Mickey, with all the pleasantries accorded to heroes, Jack was asked to step up and say a few words. He strode to the microphone and pulled a piece of yellow-lined paper from his breast pocket. He adjusted his glasses like he always did, with his left hand, a full tuft of hair on his knuckles, and leaned forward to speak into the microphone.

"I want to thank the mayor and the town for this honor. But truly, today should be about my boys. In the forty years I have been a baseball and basketball coach, I could not possibly have wished for better. I'm thankful to all the families who supported me over the years, and I want to extend special thanks to the boys themselves, many of whom I see sitting here today. This award is for you."

He held up the large key to the town. The crowd stood in applause that lasted well beyond the time they applauded for Bernadette Thompson. Most of his boys, mostly grown men now, stood as well, clapping dutifully along with the rest of the town. What else could any of them do?

Chapter 3

Fish Brook Dam

The two lovers checked each other for ticks and other tiny pests as they stepped out from behind a large tree not far from one of the many running paths along the Merrimack River. They used this spot because of the coolness of the shade from the many trees that hung over this particular secondary trail. They were deep enough in the woods that their grunts and moans were muffled by the deep forest. Now they finished putting on their clothes and walked hand in hand back to the main trail. They came to the enormous oak that hung out over the pond produced by the dam at the conclusion of Fish Brook. The woman prodded the man to try the rope swing. He laughed at her suggestion but then wanted to show off. He was about to take the rope in his hands and run back to gain speed for his swing when he spotted an odd shape draped over the falls of the dam.

"What the hell is that? Jesus, Mary."

He took her hand and carefully led her down the bank of the steep hill until they were almost standing in the pond. Carefully, they made their way along the bank, holding on to branches from the other trees that sprang up from the dank soil. When they were closer to the dam, they noticed crows fluttering about the concrete. A putrid stench hit them, almost knocking them backward. The sun was high above them and the heat near the dam increased its intensity. It certainly elevated the stink. The man stepped onto the dam and the crows flew off, complaining. The noise of their beating wings was magnified by the natural amphitheater of the steep hill that surrounded the pond and the concrete façade of the water treatment plant. As both lovers stepped closer to the form, the smell overpowered them, knocking them back and almost into the river. They wretched in unison. When the woman was able to control herself, she took one step closer. A naked body lay draped over the dam's spillway. It was bloated, with deep gashes on its legs and arms and face. Now she realized why the crows were so perturbed. She and her lover had disturbed a meal.

"Don't look, Tom," which of course made him look.

He took a step closer and saw that the eyes had been pecked out and blood had streamed down the rounded side of the dam. Some of it had washed into the Merrimack. At this spot, the river ran listlessly, so the blood mingled with the stagnant water, creating a thin, pink film that floated along with some of the green algae that formed in that spot. Tom turned and wretched again. In between stomach heaves, he shouted out, "Call 9-1-1, Mary!" She had already taken out her cellphone to make the call.

"Yes, ma'am. There's a dead man on the dam where Fish Brook meets the Merrimack. Yes, in West Beaumont. I can see a road from here. I think it comes out on River Road, not far from the Bagooian's farm. Yes, we'll stay here."

The woman grabbed Tom's arm.

"They don't want us to leave."

She took him by the hand and led him back across the dam to where they could sit along the bank and wait for the police, far enough away where the stench was not too powerful. Before they moved off, the man reached into his cut-off jeans and took out his phone, snapping a picture as the two of them tiptoed along the crest of the dam. Crows fluttered nearby, hoping to finish their feast before raccoons from the forest could steal it from them.

High overhead, two buzzards spiraled down, induced by the scent that now circulated upwards. The man uploaded his photo to Instagram and Twitter, and then finally to Facebook. Within seconds, his photo shot through the ether and was seen by thousands of his followers, who then retweeted or shared his post until thousands gawked at the deformed, bloated, dead man. When the two of them had made it back to the bank of the steep hill, Tom looked closely at the photo and realized that as he took this pic, one of the crows had landed on the thigh of the man, digging deep into his flesh, cawing to keep other crows away.

Quickly, Tom's followers responded, and news of the dead man was retweeted or shared multiple times. However mysteriously the dead man had ended up here, the world now knew about it. The corpse of the man was now entertaining or horrifying or at least interesting to millions of people, mindlessly addicted like laboratory chimps pressing levers for another piece of fruit. He didn't think of the recklessness of his actions. This is what you do when you see anything; post it and stand back and never consider the repercussions.

Chapter 4
The Chief

Police Captain Louise Consola sat at her desk in her office, not far from the place where the hometown hero ceremony had just concluded. She had just ended a phone conversation with the head of public works. Their people were busy cleaning the park after the celebration. She checked her phone again, using a police app that showed the precise location of all of her officers. It was another quiet Saturday in Beaumont, from all accounts. A couple of teenagers had been pulled over for using a phone while driving. There was a report of a car that had been broken into the night before. Nothing was stolen since the car alarm had functioned properly.

Her twin daughters, Gretchen and Pammy, were with their dad, Hank, for the day, off at Hampton Beach probably playing video games at Playland or body surfing with other families. No sharks had been reported today, thankfully, so the crowds at Hampton were their usual number. There was nothing worse for the traffic at Hampton Beach than to be engorged by the spectacle of a shark breaching and mauling a seal. Today, the people at the beach would have to be content with simply baking themselves or overeating or maintaining constant connectivity to the internet. Heaven forbid they might actually miss something.

Louise stood up from her desk and walked over to the coffee

machine. She poured herself a mug and took a careful sip, making sure not to burn the roof of her mouth. She stepped out of her office and looked down the hallway. She moved past a couple of officers doing paperwork. Eventually, she walked down to Mickey Cumming's office. He wanted his office close by so if anything big happened in town, he would find out about it right away and be one of the first people at the scene. Mayors need to be seen if they are going to be appreciated, he always thought. A vote was always a vote.

"Ceremony went well."

Louise held her cup of coffee to her lips as she leaned against the door of Mickey's office.

"It did. Big crowd."

Mickey wrote on some papers before he turned away from her and began to work on his laptop. He typed away as Louise stood in his doorway.

"You don't seem happy about the day, Mick. Surely a man of your stature loved the celebration."

"No, it was a good day," Mickey spoke without enthusiasm.

"Something bothering you, Mick?"

"Just too much paperwork. Anything going on in town I should know about?"

He looked up.

"No votes to chase today, Mick. I'm sure this will be just another sleepy Saturday in the Merrimack Valley."

"Sure," he looked back down to his laptop and continued

his two-finger typing. He was done talking. Louise got the not-so subtle hint and took another sip of her coffee before she turned away and walked back toward her office. She thought Mickey was slimy. She had known him since they were kids, swimming in Fish Brook Pond and racing their bikes in the woods by the river. He always seemed like he needed attention. Maybe that's why he became mayor. Slimy, but what politician wasn't? She kind of grunted as she walked back into her office, like she was confirming something she had always known. She sat back down at her desk and began to work on some overtime forms. Her phone beeped and she saw that it was her daughter, Pammy, sending a text.

"Have you seen this yet, mom?" Louise clicked on the twitter image. The location tab said "Beaumont" and there in all its gore was a pic of a naked, dead man being pecked at by a crow at the Fish Brook Dam. Louise looked at it in horror until she finally snapped out of the awfulness of the image and reacted to the text.

"Delete it NOW!" the chief tweeted back furiously.

She checked her app to see which officer was closest. Just then, she received a text from dispatch that a dead body had been seen at Fish Brook and Jepson was responding. The fire department and EMTs were on their way. "Why do I have to always hear about what's going on in town through the internet? Christ." Louise checked the desk drawer for the keys to her cruiser and left quickly. Her secretary repeated the report of the dead body to Chief Consola as she left her office. She walked in the other direction from Mickey Cumming's office. He could find out from someone else.

"Got it. I'll text you as soon as I see what's going on. Get a cruiser over by River Road to keep people away. Now that this is on social media, idiots from everywhere will want to see."

She made sure her gun was secured properly as she walked out the back of the station and opened the door to her cruiser. The West Beaumont section of town was about five miles from the police station. "What a fucking big town," she thought as she started up her cruiser and moved quickly out of the parking lot, heading for West Beaumont and whatever horrific scene she was about to encounter.

She had seen her share of horror as she moved up the ranks. As a state trooper, she had seen bodies crushed and unrecognizable after head-on collisions, and she had witnessed what happens when someone gets shot in the head, the gore spilling out in its gruesomeness. Part of why she advanced in her career was her ability to stay calm even during the worst carnage or most delicate domestic situation. She had her chance at being a higher-up in the Massachusetts state police, but her family grew and she decided that she wanted to see her kids grow up.

Hank had a good job as an engineer at one of the tech firms sprouting up around Boston. When the chief of police position opened in Beaumont, she applied without hesitation. Of course, she had to go through the process of being interviewed by the police board and the mayor, but she was a local and a talented one at that. This was now her tenth year on the job in the town where she was raised and she loved it, in spite of the lack of action. It seemed that that was about to change.

She drove her cruiser down North Main Street until she went through Shawsheen Village and then over to route 495. She got on the north ramp and gunned the engine for the short distance it took until she turned onto route 93 North. It was just one mile to the River Road exit, near the Vocational School and Valley's Steak House. She turned right on the exit and raced over the overpass. Her cruiser clocked 60 mph when she took the hard left curve that brought her in front of the Bagooian farm stand. One of the town cruisers was already set up by the access road to the dam. She slowed down and saw that it was Jepson, standing next to his cruiser, red directional flashlights in both hands, directing traffic, keeping curious drivers from turning down the access road.

"Did you go by the dam?"

"No, Betty is down there. I set up here as soon as I arrived, chief. The fire truck and the EMTs are already there. "

"Good. I want no one going down this road."

"No worries, chief."

Jepson resumed his duties. Traffic began to back up. People are always curious when police lights flash. And by now, some of the people in traffic had seen the gory pic. Vultures aren't limited to animals that fly. Other idiots would sneak down to the dam and more pics would flood social media. That needed to be contained, although she thought that once the picture was out, there would be no getting that horse back into the barn. She took a deep breath, nodded at Jepson, and began her drive down to the dam.

Chief Consola eased her cruiser into the intersection of

River Road and the access road to the dam. She accelerated, pushing her cruiser back up to sixty. Gravel spit from under the wheels as the cruiser took the big bend that led down to the dam. She looked to her right and saw verdant corn fields, rows and rows of tomato plants, squash, carrots, peas, and broccoli. Good New England food, keeping the Merrimack Valley alive. She rolled by some itinerant farmers, toiling in the fields, bent over in July's dispassionate blaze. She felt a trickle of moisture begin to seep into her short-sleeve uniform and down the length of her spine, soaking the small of her back and into the crack of her backside, all in spite of the cruiser's air conditioner jacked to the limit. She eased around a bend overlooking the pond. She could clearly see the rope swing that she and Hank had used many times in the days of their youth, when Townies came to swim and fish and race their bikes recklessly on the trails. Some of her best memories were made right here.

She took a deep breath and parked her cruiser next to the entrance to the water treatment plant. Betty had made sure to cordon off a place for the chief as close to the scene as possible. Louise stepped out of the cruiser. She took a deep breath, readying herself for what she was about to encounter. She made her way along the back of the treatment plant, along the familiar spillway that separated the brook from the river. Two EMTs squatted near a tarp. Crows sat on overhanging branches, wishing in vain for these horrid humans to finish their business and let them get back to their meal. They cawed at the chief as she carefully stepped onto the dam and moved toward the tarp. The EMTs were from the West Beaumont fire station. They had been the first to respond and since they were closer to the scene, the downtown Beaumont EMTs let them have this call. A lone firetruck idled on the access road. Three firefighters were taking off their bulky fireproof jackets. They were not needed and were readying themselves to leave. Their Beaumont Fire Department t-shirts were fully soaked from the late afternoon swelter that wafted up from the access road and the concrete of the dam.

Chief Consola took a few steps forward. The EMTs stood back a bit. The first thing she did was look around at the familiar landscape of her childhood play area. She reflexively looked up and back toward the high bank where the rope swing hung conspicuously under the massive oak bow. She saw herself holding on desperately to that rope years ago, only willing to let go when she swung back on firm ground. In spite of the taunts of her friends, she had never been brave (or stupid) enough to be the first one to let go and plummet into the pond. She glanced to the left a bit, over her shoulder, and made a note of the fact that the runway from the oak and the swing was still clear. Kids in town had obviously continued to play hooky by the swing. She was sure they still stole down here without their parents' permission. Minus a person jumping out of an airplane, she assumed the body had swung out over the dam and let go.

She reached into her fanny-pack and pulled out a pair of azure-colored plastic gloves. She pulled them tight up her hands and snapped the elastic against her wrist. She first lifted one side of the tarp and exposed two swollen, ashen feet. The blood had pooled on the top of the feet since the body must have ended up face down when it came to its sudden stop. She pulled the tarp a bit higher and saw the first signs that birds had been at the body. Most people assume that you look at the face of the victim first. She wasn't trained that way. You work your way up, not down. She looked closely at the multiple gashes where the birds had torn into the dark meat of the leg. She noticed plenty of blood on the dam and around the legs, but nothing was oozing out of the wounds by this point. She took the tarp and placed it back over the legs. Now she squatted next to the torso.

Lifting up the tarp, she saw massive chest injuries. There weren't any peck markings here. The birds had settled on thigh meat for their appetizer. She carefully reached under the torso and rolled the body slightly to the left and then the right. She could see shattered ribs and a crushed breastbone, nothing she didn't expect. She glanced down slightly to make sure that in fact, this was a man she was examining. Clearly, it was. Keeping mental notes, she stood up and carefully made her way to the part of the body that remained hidden under the tarp. She squatted down again. This was the hard part. She carefully took hold of the tarp and gently lifted it up. The face of the dead man had been smashed at impact. The head lay on its left side, exposing a gaping hole where the dead man's eye used to be. Most of the blood that had oozed down the side of the dam came from the man's massive head injuries. She looked at him dispassionately, the way she was trained to do. She had seen many dead men and women before. Taking it all in and maintaining calm was the way she was trained and how she was certainly going to perform her duties now.

She took her right hand and turned the head slightly,

exposing two fractured cervical vertebrae that had broken through the skin. Somehow, she noticed, the jugular vein had not been punctured or the gory scene on the dam would have been incomprehensible. She returned the head to its original if not grotesque position. The man's hair was not short but clearly wasn't very long either. She moved her hand along the hairline at the man's neck, gently lifting the hair, looking for hidden fractures. As her hand came to the neckline behind the right ear, she froze. A small, dark-blue tattoo stood in contrast to the white skin of the man's neck. She sucked the air in her lungs and held it there. The tattoo was of a basketball player shooting a jump shot. It couldn't have been more than two inches in height, allowing for the dead man's hair to cover it partially. It could only be seen if someone were looking beneath the back of the man's hairdo, like it was a tattoo the man was proud of and ashamed to see all at once. She let go of the man's hair and fell back, almost falling over the edge of the dam and into the pool of blood. The two EMTs rushed over and grabbed onto Chief Consola as she began to swoon.

"You ok, Chief?"

The female EMT jumped behind the chief and used her knees as support so the chief wouldn't fall. The male EMT held on to Chief Consola's hands. He reached into his fanny pack and brought out a metallic water bottle.

"Drink this, chief, slowly."

He undid the cap from the water bottle, handing it to her. She took two quick sips before handing the bottle back precisely, like she had to force herself to adjust her hands so she wouldn't drop the bottle. The water helped her eyes refocus and her head from spinning off into space. She felt a tremble in her gut. She knew the feeling well, usually able to keep the quivering under control when she saw something horrific, like the sight of the man's eye being pecked out. But this was more. The quaver became a wave of nausea. The chief rolled to her left and wretched uncontrollably. The female EMT held Louise's shoulders firmly. She wretched five or six times into the river, disturbing the film of blood. It made a sickly pool that when she looked at it between heaves, made her wretch over and over again.

"Easy, Chief. I've got your shoulders so you're safe. Let it come out. No one's watching except Fred and me."

For some reason, the female EMT thought it important to protect the chief's dignity by reminding her that no one had seen her toss her cookies except herself and her partner. Like that would make it better for the chief.

"I'm good," she panted. "Christ, I'm ok."

Chief Consola coughed a few times to clear the bile from her throat, spitting the residue onto the concrete that sloped down to the river. She pulled herself up with the help of the EMTs. She had to shake her head a couple of times until the image crystallized in her frontal cortex and the understanding of the enormousness of what she had just seen formed fully in her consciousness. Having regained her composure, as best she could, she reached forward and checked under the man's hair again, like she chose not to believe what it was she saw and needed some final verification, but what she saw was no mistake. She knew the man. She stood up, reaching for her smartphone. She walked to the far end of the dam, somewhat closer to where the two lovers sat huddled on the bank of the steep hill. She punched in the familiar number and the satellite connection was almost immediate.

"Hank, my God, Hank, you've got to come back, come back to Fish Brook dam."

"Go down to the side of the court. Maybe Larry Bird will sign your programs. I'll get some popcorn. Go on. I'll be here when you get back." He moved up the aisle until he entered the Loge entrance and found himself a concession stand. He bought three cones of popcorn, two cokes and a beer. *When he turned back to reenter the Loge, his right hip bumped into someone trying to step back into the garden. He had to step aside quickly so his hardness wouldn't be noticed.*

Chapter 5

Dead Oak's Crater

Chief Consola ended her text knowing her husband would return it soon. He was as calm as she was when things in their lives became tense, like the time both of the twins got injured at the same soccer game or when he had that scare with cancer ten years ago. He held up well, making sure he showed strength for his twin daughters, but Louise knew her husband could let his emotions seep through, especially late at night when they were both tired and their tongues became loose and too many things needed to be said. He could snap at her so easily when he got tired, but always, he made sure that nothing broke them apart before they fell asleep. He would keep her up until they talked out everything on his mind.

She loved him for it, but sometimes she wished he would just say he was sorry and shut the hell up so they could both get to sleep. She never held the kind of grudge where the marriage suffered because things didn't get said right at the moment. She could put it aside until it was the right time to share, but usually, Hank wanted things out in the open. The next morning, they would hold each other before they got out of bed, bad breath and all. Still, Louise couldn't fathom how her husband would handle the enormousness of his best friend, naked, dead, and pecked apart by crows, sprawled on the same dam that the three of them played on for most of their childhoods. Hell, she loved Ken almost as much as Hank loved him. They were all that close growing up. Truthfully, Louise had a bigger crush on Ken when she was in middle school. It wasn't until senior year when Hank showed interest. Their fire blazed quickly and they knew they would marry even before they both went off to college.

The chief snapped out of it. She needed to talk with the kids who called in what they saw. She knew asking the questions was going to be hard enough. She needed to keep her focus on her job. Now was not the time to wonder why Ken was dead on the dam. The river drifted past and shimmered in the late afternoon's blazing sun, and as the Chief walked away from Ken's body, a waft of stench began to swirl in the late afternoon heat. Ken was rotting away under the tarp as the temperature hovered near 90. She beckoned for Betty.

"Make sure you put the crime scene tape everywhere around the dam. Walk up the bank over there and put tape over by the top of the hill. Run the tape as far as you can along both ends of the path up by the rope swing. Call Quentin to come down here to help. Call Mike and Tamara and get them down here as well. Dammit, get everyone down here," she raised her voice and took a step backward and turned to use her phone to make the call.

She knew when her chief wanted something done immediately, and this was certainly one of those times.

She walked over to where the two lovers sat huddled on the bank almost directly under the rope swing that hung from the enormous oak. They held hands silently as the chief tight-roped across the dam. She kneeled down on the soft bank surrounding the pond and reached around to her backpack and pulled out a thermos of cold water. Mostly composed now, she handed it to the man sitting on the bank. He clearly looked like he could use a drink, but Chief Consolas had none of that kind on hand, although she did keep a bottle in her desk for when the job carried her late into the night.

"Thank you," the man spoke slowly as he handed the thermos back to the chief.

"Let's take your time with this. I know you're shook up about what you've seen. What's your name?"

"Dan Martin."

The chief looked over to the man's partner.

"Lisa Gonzales."

Louise thumbed both names and their phone numbers and addresses into her smartphone.

"Who would like to start?"

Louise looked at both Dan and Lisa. She smiled just a little bit, better to help them along with what was sure to be hard for them.

"It was the crows. There were so many of them. They sat on him and pecked at him until we scared them off," Lisa spoke first as Dan reached over and took more water from Louise's thermos.

He wasn't ready to speak. Louise could see his chest rise and fall quickly. He was spooked. Why wouldn't he be?

"Where were you before you came down to the dam?"

"Up on the bank, over by the thicket of trees, not far from the fallen oak."

"Why were you up there?" Louise turned to Dan hoping to draw him out.

"We were making out."

"In the woods? And when did you come down the bank?"

"Around 2:30. It was hot. We thought we might jump in the pond to cool off."

Dan spoke in a low voice like whatever it was he was now telling hurt him to tell it. Lisa put her arm around Dan and pulled him closer. She took over from there.

"We didn't know what we were looking at until the birds flew off when we got on the dam. Fuck. His eye was gone."

"Did you see anything before you came down the bank? Anything that might have given you pause?"

"We came out of the bushes and got dressed. We walked by this old, huge tree that was pushed over. It had this rotting stink to it, like too many dead leaves. I remember Dan turning his head away as we passed it. We noticed a water bottle and a backpack by the rope swing. We figured someone put it down during a hike. We slid down the bank and we were about to take off our clothes and jump in the pond when we saw the crows."

"And you saw nothing else? No one else around? No car? Any unusual sounds?"

Dan looked up.

"Just the seaplanes taking off and landing, across the river in Dracut. Christ."

He stopped talking like maybe he was done trying to think about what he had seen.

"OK. I'm going to have officer Betty ask you some more questions and then you can go. Betty, can you follow up with these two? I'm going up to the rope swing to look around."

Betty came over. She was rolling up the rest of the yellow crime-scene tape as she moved past the tarp with Ken's body lying beneath. She took out her own cell phone and continued to ask questions. Dan and Lisa stood up to stretch before Betty asked them to sit back down. She squatted next to them, just like Louise had done, and carried on with the morbid task of filling in the details.

Louise moved to her left along the bank and began to climb up the steepest part of the hill, directly under the spot where she and Ken and Hank and Mickey and so many people had swung out over the pond. She stumbled about halfway up, having to grab onto a tree root that protruded from deep within the rich, black soil leading to the top. Finally, she was able to haul herself up and over the top of the bank. Her uniform was covered in black soil and wood chips and other debris from the climb. She gathered herself, looking out over the precipice of the high bank, down to where she could see the extending yellow tape that Betty had strung well away from Ken's body.

She pulled her backpack off, placing it on the take-off spot for the rope swing. Her breathing was coming under control, but it was terribly hot on top of the bank, and her uniform now showed sweat stains under her pits and along her neckline and down the small of her back. She was a fit woman, but the exertion of the climb made her uniform pants chafe her thighs. She reached around and adjusted her pants so her underwear could be repositioned. She hoped no one noticed, but it was still and quiet on top of the bank by the rope swing.

She began to rotate her body counterclockwise, using her peripheral vision to spot anything level with her eyesight. Then she lowered her eyes incrementally, about five degrees in each rotation until she was looking almost straight down. It was then that she noticed a smartphone. The phone was leaning against a rock about twenty feet away from the rope swing launch point. A glint of light reflected off the phone's screen. She was surprised she hadn't noticed it as soon as she reached the summit of the steep bank. Instinctively, she understood that the phone placed in this exact spot mattered. Cell phones weren't casually tossed aside.

She stepped a few feet to her right and moved closer to the phone. She bent down and looked closely. She didn't want to touch it, but the phone seemed placed there at an angle so someone would see it eventually. She took hold of the backpack and looked through it to see if there was anything within. Nothing. Then she froze in place. She looked around in the gathering dusk and saw, mingled with her shoe prints, there were two other sets of prints. She cursed at herself. She had let the distraction of the phone and the backpack disturb her concentration, and now she knew she had spoiled the scene by walking among the other prints. She squatted down again. One of the sets of prints was clearly that of running shoes. The other prints were of someone's bare feet.

"Well I'm a jackass." She reached for her own cell phone and called down to Betty. "I'm going to need help up here. Can you contact the state police? I think I've spoiled the scene. I'm going to stay up here until they get here."

She squatted so her backside almost touched the ground. She noticed that the running shoe and barefoot prints headed off along the path south toward Tewksbury and the old seminary. She knew this path well. There were no prints coming from the Beaumont side of the trail, back into the neighborhoods and down toward River Road. At least that would make the search of the area a bit easier.

She eased herself closer to the ground, setting herself in a push up position to let her body and face hover as close to the phone as possible. She examined it carefully. Its glass protector was perfect, like it had never been used before. Again, she noticed that the angle of the phone was set perfectly so that if someone wanted to record a video or take a picture of the rope swing launch point, it had been placed there properly to do so. She was relieved that she had not been stupid enough to touch the phone, even though she was still disgusted with herself for spoiling the area with her own footprints. "Fuck," she thought to herself. Off in the distance she heard the wail of police cars traveling down the access road to the dam. She stood back up. Three state police cars slowed and parked near the dam. Four troopers got out. Betty had moved Dan and Lisa away from the body and across the dam to the access road. One of the state troopers took out a small notepad and began jotting something down, while Betty and the other three made their way around the water-treatment facility and stepped onto the dam.

They stopped by Ken's body. Two of the troopers squatted down and looked under the tarp and started making notes. Betty and the last trooper walked along the dam and over to the path at the base of the steep hill. Louise could see Betty point up the hill. The trooper walked away from Betty and reaching the base of the hill, began to climb up the steep bank. He scurried up quickly, surprising Louise with how much faster he reached the summit than she had. She reminded herself that she needed to spend more time in the gym, an odd thought right then. When he reached the top, Louise held out her hand in a stop sign.

"I'm Chief Louise Consola, Beaumont police. Stay right in that spot. I've already spoiled the scene with my footprints. I'll come to you."

"Captain Bill Gallagher, State Police. I'll stay right here."

Louise carefully retraced her steps toward the rope swing. She shook hands with Gallagher.

"Who's the dead guy?" Gallagher asked.

"Friend of mine and my husband. Ken Richardson. We grew up together in town, raced our bikes on these paths. Swam in the pond. Swung on this rope."

Louise gestured toward the still-hanging rope, motionless in the stagnation of Beaumont's late-afternoon heat.

"Jesus."

"I need your help. I've spoiled the scene already. Can you help me look around? I'll walk along the edge of the path in the leaves and pine needles. Would you mind looking closely at the phone and maybe get one of your people up here to look at the footprints?" Louise pointed down toward the cellphone and around in a circular motion.

"One of my guys will come up. I'll have him check the footprints. I'll retrace your steps and look at the phone. Do what you have to do. Christ, this is awful for you."

"Yes. Thank you."

Louise took a quick spring to her left and landed in the pine needles and dead leaves on the side of the path farthest away from the rope swing. She began walking slowly in the direction of where the footprints came, deeper into the forest and almost down to the steep, rocky plunge that made this part of the path so difficult for runners. Not far from the descent, an old oak tree lay upended, the ball of its roots clearly visible, extending bony fingers deep into a dark pit, like an old man reaching out, desperate, holding on to life, long-since misused. Louise slowly walked past the hole and peered forward toward the rocky outcropping where the footsteps disappeared.

She looked down at the granite bank. How many times had she and Hank and Ken and Mickey and the rest of their friends played here, racing up the formidable hill, unfazed by its severity, overwhelming the steep climb with the vigor of their youth, hand over hand, climbing until someone won the race to the top? That usually meant that whoever was last would have to be the first to swing out over the pond and drop into the springtime cold or summer's languid warmth. Then all of them would float and bob and splash each other, and nothing of the kind of things they would encounter later in life would matter or even entertain the dark possibilities of their futures. The hills and the trails and the rocks and the rope swing and the pleasantly deep pond was home and to them, at the time, it could not possibly be disturbed.

Those adolescent views of the future were split asunder now to Louise, and soon for her husband, once he arrived on the scene. Louise didn't know how she could break the awfulness of Ken's death to Hank, but right now, she needed to clear those thoughts from her mind and attend to the details of the surroundings.

She began to retrace her path through the leaves and pine needles when she picked up a flash of color with her peripheral vision. Deep in the crater left by the overturned oak, she noticed a ball of clothes. She must have missed them when she looked out over the steep granite drop. They seemed to be tied up with something. She stepped carefully, squatting down to see if there were any footprints. There were.

A set of running shoe prints moved along the dusty path, out toward the rope swing about fifty feet away. She scanned the crater and noticed barefoot prints leading from the rope swing to the crater and then back in the same direction. She looked slightly past the root ball and picked up a long stick. She took hold and stretched out her arm, carefully prodding the clothes ball. Lifting it toward her. She dropped it down next to her and discarded the stick. She lay almost on her side and getting as close to the clothes as possible, she examined them carefully. She could see what looked like running gear: a long-sleeved running shirt, some running shorts, and some worn out, white running socks. They were tied together by a pair of white shoelaces. The colors of the tied-up clothes were mostly subdued, but a flash of gold stuck out from within. She reached over and picked the stick back up and moved the outer clothes around until she could make out what looked like a pair of kid's sneakers.

She pushed a bit more until she could see a distinct, gold star on the ankles of the shoes. It was the star that was familiar to everyone she grew up with; a Converse All-Star. A sick feeling grew over her. This pair of shoes looked like the same gold Converse All-Star basketball shoes Hank and Ken wore when they played youth basketball. Hank had hung on to his sneakers, like a family heirloom that he couldn't or wouldn't discard. So the ball of clothes and running shoes and All-Stars had to be Ken's. He must have tied them up and tossed them into the tree's crater before he swung out and killed himself. But why?

"Gallagher, can you come over here? Walk along the pines," Louise shouted. She shimmied back into her crouched position but made sure not to move onto the footprints or disturb the clothes bundle. "I have something."

Gallagher walked along the pines. He was wearing rubber gloves and he held the smartphone in his hands.

"So do I. There's a video, Chief. You're not going to like it."

The ride home was loud. Ken and Hank raved about the play of

Larry Bird. Jack drove his car into McDonald's and bought three orders of cheeseburgers, fries, and chocolate shakes. "Let's eat somewhere else," he turned to Hank and Ken, sitting in the back seat, as he passed the food back to them. "Let's go eat somewhere where we can talk about the game without being interrupted." The boys ate their burgers and fries and sucked on their shakes and drove off with Jack, thinking nothing was unusual. There was a parking lot behind the grocery store down the street. It would be quiet enough, Jack thought to himself.

Chapter 6

The Video

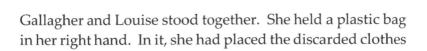

Gallagher and Louise stood together. She held a plastic bag in her right hand. In it, she had placed the discarded clothes and gold basketball sneakers.

"Can you take these and check them for prints and DNA? You guys will do it faster than my people can."

"Of course."

They picked a spot in the gathering gloom, set back into the forest, not more than ten feet from the path. They made sure to step through leaves and pine needles so as not to disturb the footprints now being worked on by Gallagher's men.

Gallagher wore a pair of opaque rubber gloves. He held out the phone. He hit the play button and a surprisingly vivid image of Ken Richardson appeared. They both listened to the cryptic message before Ken placed the video camera on what was apparently the same rock where the smartphone was found. They could both hear what sounded like clothes being taken off, and then footsteps moving off and then returning, and then the image of a naked man swinging over the pond and coming back. The smartphone angle was then turned and once again, the image of Ken Richardson could be seen swinging, this time at a slightly different angle off the cliff and out toward the river and the dam below. They stood watching in horror as Ken's body plummeted from the apex of his swing and crashed full onto the dam. The collision with the concrete was so powerful that the body bounced directly back from the direction it fell and then slammed, face first onto the suddenness of the dam. It lay motionless in the midday sun. The lifeless river moved ponderously beyond, seemingly unaware of the tragedy.

They rewound the video, and then once more. They stood touching shoulders, although they probably would not have noticed, so intensely did they watch Ken's death. They were startled out of their focus when they both heard a scream coming from the dam. Louise knew the voice. It was Hank. He had arrived and stupidly, the state trooper by Ken's body hadn't kept Hank away. Louise handed the phone to Gallagher and raced to the cliff and slid down the embankment. To hell with the footprints and the crime scene. She raced along the base of the cliff and sprinted over the dam, half-blinded by the sun, now low on the horizon. She almost tackled her husband. She drove him off and away from the unzipped body bag and held him as he struggled to get free.

"He's gone. Don't look at him like this, Hank. He's gone."

She held his face in her hands and tried to pull him close. His body began to sag and she had to use all of her strength to keep him upright, but after a moment, she let him slide to the edge of the dam, a good fifteen feet away from Ken. The two of them rocked back and forth. Hank let out repeated wails. His shoulders shook and the echoes of his cries scared a flock of crows off their nearby perch, probably the same crows who feasted on Ken earlier in the day. By now, Gallagher and his men had climbed down the hill and moved to Ken's body, zipping the bag slowly so the sound wouldn't disturb Louise and Hank.

There was just enough room on the dam for them to carefully carry Ken's body toward the other end of the dam and the coroner's wagon parked nearby. Gallagher spoke quietly. He said that he'd be in his office all night and for Louise to call when she was ready. She shook her head slightly in recognition as she continued to hold her husband. The flock of crows flew back and settled again on the branches of a nearby tree. They looked down at the chief and her husband. The river moved along on its ignorant, unremitting course.

"What a game! Larry Bird couldn't miss." Jack Monroe turned in his seat and looked back at the boys. They sat together, stuffing fries in their mouths. "One of you come up and sit with me in the front. I'm not a taxi driver." Ken and Hank looked at each other. Hank shook his head. Ken stuck his fries back into the McDonald's bag. He jumped out of his seat in the back and squirmed past Hank into the front seat of Jack's small car. He took out his cheeseburger and took a large bite. He sucked on his straw and washed down the burger with some of his shake. Jack reached over and patted Ken's knee. "What a great night," was all he said. Hank sat in the back and held his breath. His young muscles tensed. The back of the car seemed very dark to him, sitting by himself as something unfolded in front of him that he did not understand.

Chapter 7

Mickey D's

Jack Monroe sat on his porch. His house was set well back away from traffic. A quiet lot, hidden by tangled trees and overgrown brush. Veiled. He adjusted his thick glasses. The rubber band held them firmly against his balding head. His hands had not been washed. Axle grease and brake fluid stained his hairy fingers. He swiped through some of his special downloads on his phone. It was more difficult for him to get aroused now that he was older, but that didn't stop him from trying. He held his gaze on an Asian nine-year-old. He reached down and undid his zipper. His inground pool reflected the setting sun.

His Instagram account beeped. There was a picture of a dead man, draped on a dam. A single crow worked at the man's leg. The location tag said Beaumont, he noticed. He looked more carefully. It was a picture of the dam. The dam at Fish Brook. Not far from the upturned oak. His place. Coincidence, of course. Still, he lingered on the Instagram pic. There had already been one hundred-thousand likes, and there was something oddly familiar about the dead man. He took his thumb and index finger and zoomed in on the picture. He adjusted the focus toward the dead man's neck. There was the faintest image of a tattoo. A basketball player shooting a jump shot. That was Ken's tattoo. He remembered Ken showing it off with his buddy, Hank.

They were so proud to be the first ones in their grade to get tattoos.

Hank begged to be driven home first, that dark night after the Celtics game. He was headstrong, that one, and not easy prey. Ken was weaker, easier. His dad wasn't around much, and the mom enjoyed drinking. He needed a father figure. That certainly played in his favor.

Jack's mind drifted back to the unmistakable aroma of French fries as he slipped back to that first night. His toad mind squirmed. Ken had been his favorite, at least until he was used up and someone else became available, another, too weak to see the trap or too needy to notice being groomed, too naive and then in too deep, brutalized and destroyed and shamed into silence. It had worked before and it would work again. No reason to believe otherwise, after years of success. Just another boy at the root ball.

But Ken was dead today, on Jack's day, his hometown hero day, such a disgrace to have the attention drawn away, in such an unfair manner. His amphibious brain continued to work at it, livid and vile.

But Hank was still alive. Jack knew that Ken and Hank were best friends. They shared everything. Maybe too much. Nothing was going to ruin the honor of being a hometown hero. Nothing, not the least of which was little Hank Consola, the elusive fish. He needed to be attended to.

He would need to retrieve some tools from the garage. Cutting tools. An easy snip or two and little Hank Consola would be silenced. He would get his, the thing he truly deserved, the one that got away. It would be easy, a neighborhood emptied by mourners on the day of the funeral, a loose end cauterized.

The gold metal hung against his chest. Mickey Cummings knew, but he'd kept quiet all these years. Jack had a video so he knew the mayor would stay buttoned up. Still, something to consider. Insurance policy. First thing, though, he needed to cut the wires. Obviously the first thing. He thought about it for a moment, then swiped back to the Asian boy.

Chapter 8

Cold Lasagna

Gretchen took out plates and silverware and began to set the table. Pammy took out some left-over pizza and macaroni and cheese and heated both in the microwave. She stared at the timer as it slowly ticked down. The timer beeped, startling her dad from whatever deep place he had just been. He looked out the window to the family patio and the grill where he and Ken had spent so much time. Louise sat across from her husband. She was out of her police uniform. She wore khaki shorts and a blue "Beaumont Warrior" t-shirt. Her black flip flops hung slightly off of her feet. She had her legs crossed and her left foot moved nervously.

The flip flop defied gravity and somehow remained precariously on the end of her toes. Her flip flops falling to the floor would have been another brutal noise to startle her husband. She kept the delicate balance as she waited for her husband to turn and face her. After the long, painful funeral, five days after Ken's death, Hank remained in a daze. He had said very little leading up to the funeral and burial. He stood silently as the preacher said all the right words. None of them broke through Hank's concrete façade and he had hung onto it tightly, right up to this moment.

Gretchen and Pammy sat down and waited for their

parents to reach out to them and hold hands for their mealtime prayers. No one moved. Louise finally reached over to her daughters and they took their father's hand and she began.

"Dear heavenly father, we ask for your blessings this day and for the food you have presented before us. Watch over all our family and our friends, those with us and those since departed. Yeah, though we walk in the shadow of death, we fear no evil."

Louise kept her head bowed, allowing her words of prayer to sink fully into her family.

"Amen."

The four of them let go of each other's hands. The food remained untouched. The sun had set long ago, but there was still the faintest touch of light coming through the patio window. The sun's rays had long since been cut off by the horizon and a gathering darkness spread across their backyard. Only one light lit the kitchen, casting an eerie pall throughout the house. Gretchen looked at her mother and father, then to her sister, sensing that her parents might need to be alone.

"Come on. Let's eat in the living room, Pammy."

Gretchen took her plate, careful not to spill the pizza or macaroni. She pushed back her chair. It made a loud, abrupt grating sound, startling her father once again. Pammy took her plate and followed. Before she left the kitchen, she kissed her father on the top of his head, then headed to the sink where she scraped off the hardened mac and cheese. She turned on the disposal and the sound of whatever food was in the sink could be heard grinding between the blades. The noise of it reverberated through the intense quiet of their house, like a woodchipper ripping up logs and spitting them out.

"Jesus, Pammy!" Louise turned to yell at her daughter as Hank reacted with a visible shake, his shoulders bunching tight against his neck. He recovered after a few moments.

"It's alright, Louise." He turned his neck to his left and then right, trying to loosen his shoulders. "Pammy, go eat with your sister."

His daughter walked quickly out of the kitchen and down the hall to the sound of the TV playing a new Netflix drama. Both daughters balanced their plates on their legs and quickly pulled out their phones. Social media was still on fire with the news of the death of the man from Beaumont, even a week later. They flipped through their apps, past the still-brutal images of their uncle Ken and the ridiculousness of what compelled people to be mindless voyeurs. The twins turned on their YouTube app and tried to get lost in some of its inane pointlessness, at least for a while.

Louise sat and waited for her husband to speak. It had been a cripplingly long day. They sat there, exhausted to their core. Gallagher had called an hour earlier. The forensics from the state police had matched the footprints his team had collected with the footprints of Ken's running shoes and his bare feet. Not that there was any real doubt since the DNA from Ken matched the DNA from the basketball shoes.

It wasn't foul play, which both he and Louise had already

surmised. They had watched the video of Ken plummeting to his death. Still, why? Ken had never married. He hadn't dated much. That was the subject of some rumors spread indiscriminately by some people in town. Louise had long ago dismissed the speculation among some of the townsfolk. Idle gossip, that. Ken had a good job that paid well, and he was well liked by everyone in town. To Louise, his suicide was incomprehensible. Nothing added up. The main thing that still haunted her as she sat at the kitchen table, waiting for her husband to talk, was the tied-up clothes left in the crater of the root ball, especially the basketball sneakers.

And why did Ken choose to be naked when he killed himself? As a former state trooper and now chief of police, she knew a clue when she saw one, and she knew those two bizarre facts were connected. She put her thoughts aside and sat and waited for Hank to speak. She waited patiently, letting him work through his best friend's death and today's brutal funeral. She took a small bite from the lasagna. It had long-since cooled and now sat tasteless in her mouth. None of her senses worked properly after last week. Still, she waited. Finally, her husband looked up from his plate. His eyes were red from the crying and wailing after placing dirt on Ken's casket, slowly lowered into the broken earth.

She watched her husband look up, his gaze fixed on her as he seemed ready to open up. Instead, Hank took his plate of lasagna and threw it. The plate shattered and the cold pasta and red sauce slid down the side of the wall.

"Jesus!" Louise gasped, shoving her chair backwards and jumping up from the table.

The grating sound of the chair being flung backwards reverberated through the kitchen. Some of the red sauce had splattered on her face. Pammy and Gretchen raced in without their phones. They stood in horror as their dad slowly placed his head on the kitchen table. His breathing was tortured and his shoulders shook, but no sound emanated from him. His daughters remained frozen, shocked, staring at their grieving father. Louise quickly stepped around the kitchen table, wiping the sauce off of her as she approached her husband. She paused for a moment before reaching down and pulling Hank toward her. Only then did the slightest of sounds escape from him. It came out in a whisper, barely audible to Louise.

"I did this. I did all of it." Hank put his hands on his wife's strong arms and stared into her eyes. "All of it."

"What do you mean? My god, Hank."

"All of it."

He stood, breaking his wife's hold and quietly stepped away from her. He walked slowly toward the living room archway. Pammy and Gretchen moved out of the way, both of their faces set in shock. Hank reached for the car keys on the counter and opened the door leading to the garage. He walked to his car and turned on the ignition and carefully backed out. He shifted the car into drive and rolled down the driveway, turning right and heading toward the center of town, leaving his stunned and confused family behind.

The twins turned back to look at their mom, the chief of police and one of the two rocks of their world. She took a napkin and cleaned off the rest of the red sauce from her face. It looked like blood splatter after a shotgun blast.

"Go after him, mom!" Pammy finally screamed when she realized her mom wasn't budging.

"What did he mean when he said it was his fault?"

Gretchen took a step closer to her mother.

"I do not know."

Her mind raced and she kept coming back to the final image of Ken's casket being lowered into the dank earth. She thought to herself how Hank was inconsolable, almost falling on the ground at the edge of the grave. It took Pammy and Gretchen and her using all their strength to help Hank away from the cemetery. At the reception at the church, he sat by himself, barely acknowledging some of his friends who came to lend him support. Mickey Cummings sat with Hank for a long time. They did not speak to each other. It was unusual for Mickey to not be working a room, shaking hands and solidifying his position as mayor. But Louise noticed that Mickey was out of character, and as he and Hank sat by themselves, it seemed to her like there was some force that connected their mourning, that they could sit by themselves, no words between them, and still keep themselves from dissolving in front of the other mourners.

She stood in the kitchen, snapped back to the reality of what had just transpired and how it had shaken her daughters.

"He'll be back. He needs time to process all of this. It has been overwhelming for him." She looked at her daughters. "Come help me clean up."

The three of them silently labored to remove the cold lasagna splattered across the wall of their kitchen.

Chapter 9

Brake Lines

Hank drove through Beaumont, a dense fog adding a painful thickness to the night. His car slowly accelerated until he drove past McDonald's on Main Street, edging toward full speed. He glanced to his left to see the big yellow arches of McDonald's. He remembered a night after the Celtic's game years ago, eating his food with Ken at a dark parking lot not far away. For years, he had been able to keep the horror of that night repressed, but it had seeped out over the last week after Ken's death. Now the memory was stark, bursting forth from his weakness. There wasn't much strength left for Hank to hold it back.

His car sped past Tony's barber shop where most of his friends had their hair cut back in the day. He gunned the engine, racing through the red light by Harding Street. His car leaped as it bolted forward. To his right, the old Tyre Rubber factory sat silent in the dark. Its fractured windows had long since been boarded up. There was a rumor that it was going to be turned into condos and office space, just one more example of Beaumont's creeping sprawl. The factory was used back in the day to make the soles of Converse All-Stars. Many of the boys and girls in town bought their first pair of hoop shoes right there. The highlight of the trip was when the kids saw the enormous pair of Bob Lanier basketball shoes, size 23 or something

51

like that. Ken and Hank had gone together and bought shoes when they played on the same church league team, Saint Robert Bellarmine. Kids playing basketball, Hank thought to himself. Nothing could be so pure.

His car hurtled over the B&M railroad bridge. All the windows to his car were rolled down and the wind from the air blurred his vision. He wiped away the moisture from his eyes with both of his fists, letting go of the wheel for just a bit too long. Something was in the middle of the road, perhaps a raccoon. Hank barely caught a glimpse of the animal before he ran it down. He tightened his hold on the wheel, overcompensating, and lost control.

His car careened into the town's center. He struggled to regain control, but inertia had won out. He slammed his foot down and tried to hit the brakes. He pumped hard twice but his brakes would not catch. He spun the steering wheel, but the force of the turn and the speed of his car worked against him. The edges of his tires caught the asphalt. Hank's car flipped sideways, somersaulting twice. His body was tossed violently against the driver's side door and then hard into the steering wheel and up against the roof. With one last flip, the car smashed headlong into the civil war statue that sat in the town square, right by the library. The roof of his car was smashed in and the front windshield disintegrated. Hank's seatbelt did its job.

In spite of the destruction of his car, Hank was not thrown from the vehicle. He sat in the flattened wreck, stunned by the violence of the crash. There was smoke coming from the engine and the smell of gasoline was heavy. A hissing noise drifted from the engine and one of his tires rotated listlessly. His head hurt badly from when the roof smashed down onto his skull. Blood streamed down his face. His left arm was pinned against the door. A searing pain shot up from his wrist to his shoulder.

Slowly, he became conscious of his surroundings. It was deathly quiet except for the hiss coming from the engine. More smoke filled the car. He took his right hand and tried to clear off the blood that now streamed down his face. He spat and blood sprayed against the steering wheel. With his uninjured right hand, he reached down and with an effort, released the seat belt. He reached across his body and grabbed the door handle. Pushing hard, the door opened, and he tumbled out of his car. A shot of pain burst from his shattered left arm as his body crashed onto the pavement. On his stomach, using his legs and his one good arm, he crawled away from the car, maybe twenty feet. By then other cars had stopped and people ran over to him. They helped him up and carried him another ten feet when a spark ignited the gas that spilled from the engine.

The car caught fire and just as Hank was placed on the stairs leading up to the town library, the car exploded, sending a shockwave that drove Hank and his good Samaritans against the door to the library. Shards of glass flew through the air as the fireball from the explosion mushroomed into the dark, nighttime sky. The man and the woman who had helped Hank lay against the library door, unconscious. Their faces bled from the cuts from flying glass. Hank's body was flung backwards. His shirt and shorts were covered with glass. He lay on his good side, his broken arm turned at a confused angle. He felt his mind start to wobble and his consciousness begin to slide away. Ambulances and police cruisers and fire trucks arrived on the scene, but he soon lost consciousness and he drifted off to a very dark place.

The burgers and fries were eaten, and the trash was stuffed in a McDonald's bag. Hank sat in the back of Jack's car. Jack undid his seatbelt and turned to face Ken. His right leg rested against Ken's left. Jack put his arm on Ken's headrest. The talk between the two in the front seat continued on the topic of bounce passes and hook shots, footwork and defensive stances. Jack said how impressed he was with how Larry Bird could dribble between his legs. He took his arm away from the headrest and placed it on the emergency brake between him and Ken. His fingertips brushed against Ken's leg. Hank watched it all. His heart pounded. He ate a French fry, sensing a dark thing taking hold in the front of Jack's cramped car. He was too much of a boy to ask to be taken home and not enough of a man to demand it. He just knew that he wanted to be out of Jack's car and back in the safety of his own home.

Chapter 10

The Mayor of Beaumont

Mickey Cummings sat in his office. He had made it to the scene where the body of his friend, Ken Richardson, had been tagged and bagged and driven off to the coroner's office of the state police.

He wanted to talk with Louise but thought better of it. She had enough to deal with. Her husband was inconsolable. Better to let them be. He talked to a few of the state troopers who remained at the scene. He had viewed the pictures on the internet of Ken's bloated body like thousands of other people had done. At the time, he managed to hold down the sickness that stirred in his gut. The mayor of Beaumont couldn't be seen throwing up in public. He left quickly and drove back to his office. He walked in and quickly shut the door, barely making it to the wastebasket before throwing up. He shook violently as he wretched into the wastebasket next to his desk. He rested his head on his desk as he fought against the nausea. Large beads of sweat formed on his brow. Finally, he sat back up and leaned back in his chair, panting, trying to regain his composure.

What a fucking phony he was, he thought, a coward, standing on the podium and saying kind words about Jack Monroe, biting down hard on his cigar as Jack thanked the town and the boys. He found himself incredulous because in fact he was one of those boys. He thought back to a weekend trip to Cape Cod to play in a basketball tournament, years ago but still seared into his memory. There were eleven boys on the trip. When the roommates were chosen, he was the odd boy out and was forced to bunk with Jack. Ken and Hank skipped the trip that week, so he was left alone. A small part of Mickey never forgave Hank and Ken for leaving him alone on that trip, for the agony he carried even to this day, amplified to its apex now that Ken was dead.

He remembered Jack Monroe had rented some cheap hotel on the Cape for him and the boys. The rooms were tiny, and the beds covered with threadbare comforters. All the rooms smelled powerfully of mildew.

It was late in the evening when Jack reached over to Mickey. Jack was heavy and he easily pinned Mickey down on his face and held him down until it was over. Mickey was much too small to fight back against Jack's girth. He tried to squirm free, but he was helpless, not only because of the violence of the assault but the confusion of what was actually transpiring What could Mickey do? The boys in the nearby rooms might have been confused by the strange noises, but if they were, they didn't come to find out what was happening to Mickey Cummings. Either way.

He kept the secret for years. Shortly after he was elected mayor, Jack Monroe showed up in Mickey's plush office. He sat across from Mickey and slid forward a video. He claimed it was a video of Mickey Cummings leaving a Motel 6 on the outskirts of Boston, arm and arm with a man. A deep kiss, full tongue. Jack told Mickey he had been careless. How Jack was there at that exact moment didn't matter. Wouldn't it be awful for Mickey if the town saw the video?

It was the second devastating secret Mickey had to swallow, all these years later. The horror of it had become opaque, like a kitchen window in need of scrubbing, but the glass remained blurred. Sometimes it was better to not be able to see through to the outside. Better to stay behind the mired glass.

When Mickey felt weak and the evil of Jack Monroe's blackmail seeped back into the mayor's consciousness, it overwhelmed him, sending him into a prolonged funk that debilitated him for weeks. He would hole up in his home or come to work and lock the door, cancelling appointments and refusing to see constituents. Eventually, the fit would pass, but his friends saw, over time, his dark, wavy hair transform first to premature gray and now to almost complete white.

As he sat in his office, he understood that he would be taking that evil to his grave, whenever that dark pit opened up before him. The enormity of Ken's death had pushed Mickey once again to that place of weakness. Sometimes he wondered if stepping off the precipice and falling into a dark grave would be a relief. He worked hard to keep that thought at bay.

The vomit from the puke sat in the bucket next to his desk. He'd call someone eventually to take his mess away. The stench was punishment enough for Mickey, better to leave it there to add to his self-flagellation.

It was a week later, the night after the funeral, near midnight, and once again, Mickey was alone in his office. He had almost fallen asleep, an empty bottle of vodka on his desk, when his phone beeped. He was startled into consciousness and reached for the phone, looking at the text. There had been an accident on Main Street, a quarter mile from where he sat in his darkened office. He stood quickly, sobering fast. He grabbed his keys to his Lexus and stepped out of his office, the taste of the vodka still strong in his mouth. He jumped into his car and sped out of the parking lot behind the town hall.

As soon as he turned north onto Main Street, he could see fire and smoke billowing into the dark. There was a desperate wail of sirens, egging him to drive fast. He arrived at the chaotic scene within seconds. A crowd of people had already formed, held back by one of Louise's deputies, Betty, he thought. The car leaned precariously against the civil war statue in the town center. Flames had fully engulfed the car and now firemen were busy trying to douse the flames. Three ambulances were parked not far from the library. People were being loaded in, carefully but urgently. Mickey parked his car across the street and ran toward the last ambulance.

His breathing was labored from too much Chinese food and vodka and cigars. He tried to catch his breath as he leaned around the side of the ambulance. It was Hank, arm already in a sling and his shirt covered with blood. There was a thick gauze pad on his head, stained in crimson. His eyes were barely open and he moaned as the EMTs lifted the gurney and carefully slid him into the ambulance. Mickey stepped back and the ambulance sped off, back down Main Street toward Lawrence, its sirens blaring. Betty noticed Mickey. She stepped quickly over to him.

"They're bringing everyone to Lawrence General," she said in a loud voice over the din.

"Thanks, Betty. Where's Louise?"

"I already called her. They'll meet Hank at the hospital. Christ, what a fucking day. Ken's funeral and now this? Shit."

Betty stepped away. She walked over to where the mobile news crews were setting up. Another tragedy in Beaumont. Ratings through the roof. She answered questions, trying to deflect their attention away from the mayor. She wanted him to get away without being harassed by their prying questions. Mickey moved quickly back to his car, avoiding curious looks from the townspeople who had gathered at the crash. He jumped in and sped off in the direction of the hospital. He prayed that Hank was okay and this part of the town's growing nightmare would end differently than it had for Ken Richardson.

Chapter 11

Secrets

Louise sat on the edge of Hank's hospital bed. An opaque bag hung from a long, metallic stand. An occasional drip from an IV coursed down a tube connected to Hank's right arm. His left arm was elevated, encased by a cast that pumped liquid hydrogen around Hank's arm, keeping the swelling down after the doctor performed surgery to the badly broken bones.

Hank's head was heavily bandaged. Both his eyes were purple-black from the skull fracture and concussion from when Hank's head was almost crushed by the roof of his car.

Gretchen and Pammy sat in drab hospital chairs at the foot of their dad's bed. They had their faces glued to their smartphones, waiting for their father to awaken. The doctors had said their dad would be fine in time. The concussion was bad but there was no bleeding on the brain. His hard head had kept everything in place, the doctor kind of laughed. The arm was set and would heal in time. He was lucky, considering the car exploded moments after Hank had crawled free. The doctor left them alone and carried out the rest of his rounds.

Louise held her husband's hand and waited for him to come around. Ken was dead and now her husband lay unconscious. She would not cry in front of her children. She felt her job as chief of police required that much and she wanted to be strong for her girls. But she wanted to cry. It was agony losing Ken, and now Hank, her best friend and the love of her life lay in a hospital bed on the same day as they put Ken in the ground.

She tried to piece together the facts. She kept coming back to Ken's video and the clothes she found under the upturned oak. Ken had said that he had had enough, but what made it so awful that he would decide to kill himself? Why leave an old pair of kid's basketball shoes tied up and left behind in the crater of the root ball? Clearly, Ken had left the shoes there to be found. And why that day? It had been a nondescript sort of day, except for the hometown hero parade. Jack Monroe was Ken and Hank's coach in both baseball and basketball. She knew she needed to call Jack. She was pretty sure he had heard the news of Hank's accident by now, but she wanted to make sure. Fucking social media. She was exhausted as she waited for her husband to regain consciousness. The call would wait.

The door to Hank's room opened slowly. Gallagher walked in. He was trim in his all-blue Massachusetts State Police uniform. His service revolver shined blue from within its holster. He stepped into the bedroom and took off his hat.

"Is he going to be ok?"

"Gallagher, you didn't have to come over. But yes, he's ok. He's got a skull fracture and bad concussion, but there was no bleeding on the brain. His left arm is broken in two places. It took three hours to set the arm properly. The doctor said he should be coming around soon."

Gallagher leaned over. He spoke softly in Louise' ear so the girls could not hear.

"The brake lines were cut, chief."

He remained there, close to Louise, letting what he had just shared sink in.

"I'm sorry?"

"The brake lines were cut. We brought the car to the pound and one of my people checked it out. The car was badly burned, but when she checked under the chassis, she saw that the brake line had been cut. She said it couldn't have happened in the crash. The line was cut like someone knew precisely what they were doing."

"Christ, Gallagher. You're sure?"

"I am. Said there was no doubt."

Louise stood up and walked around the room, moving past Gretchen and Pammy. They sensed a change in their mother and looked up from their phones.

"What is it, mom?" Gretchen got up and stood close to her mother. Pammy joined them.

"I'll be just outside if you need me."

Gallagher excused himself and left the room. Louise looked at her daughters. They weren't kids anymore, really. What fifteen-year-old girls were these days? They had suffered this week, first their Uncle Ken's death and now their dad's crash. She decided they should know.

"Your dad's crash wasn't an accident. Someone cut the

brake lines."

Both girls' eyes widened. Gretchen put her hand up to her mouth.

"I don't understand," Pammy spoke quietly.

"We don't know anything else. Trooper Gallagher just told me. I didn't want to keep it from you. Something terrible is going on, but you are almost adults. You deserve to know."

The twins stood motionless. The air in the hospital room seemed very thin. The three of them stood looking at each other. Hank's IV continued to drip and he lay motionless on the hospital bed, cream colored blankets pulled up to his chest.

"I thought dad was trying to kill himself, mom, Jesus!" Pammy blurted out what she and Gretchen had spoken of between themselves as they waited for their father to get out of surgery.

"My god, Pammy. Why would you think that?"

"You saw how he looked when he left the house, mom. His face looked cold, like something terrible had welled up inside and it was devouring him. One second he is in a rage, throwing his plate of lasagna, and then his face morphed, like he had become possessed. It scared me. Gretchen too. Uncle Ken was like his brother and he ended up taking his life."

"Your dad would never take his own life."

"We still can't believe Uncle Ken took his." Gretchen put her arm around Pammy and pulled her close, taking her other arm and putting it around her mother's shoulders. "Can't you see why we might think that dad couldn't take it? He said it himself, that it was all his fault, right after he threw the plate. You should have gone after him, mom. Maybe you could have stopped him before he crashed."

Pammy looked accusingly at her mother.

"God damn it, that's not fair, Pammy."

"But it's true," Gretchen agreed.

"No, it's not. Stop it, both of you."

Gretchen and Pammy stepped away, bruised, and sat back down. This time they left their phones alone and looked at their unconscious father.

"I know your father. He needed time. I had to let him be."

"We know him too. I've never seen his face like that before." Gretchen's voice was thin. "Now you're saying that maybe someone wanted dad dead?"

She burst into tears and her sister quickly got out of her chair and held onto Pammy. They both cried as the magnitude of the news fully crystallized.

Louise could and would not dismiss Gallagher's information. Someone had cut the line and whoever it was knew what they were doing. She stepped forward to reach for her girls. She pulled up short. A low moan came from the bed. Hank's eyes fluttered open and he shifted his weight. The IV tugged at his arm, painfully keeping him from moving any farther. With his right hand, he reached up and touched his forehead. He looked around, trying to make sense of his surroundings. He looked at his wife who had stepped quickly to the side of the bed opposite the girls. She put her hand on Hank's chest and kissed his cheek tenderly.

"You're in the hospital. There was a crash and then a fire. You're lucky to be alive. We thought we might lose you."

Louise spoke softly, still holding in the tears that she knew she had to quash but wanted so desperately to let out. Hank took a deep breath and winced. He began to comprehend where he was. Slowly, he began to recall what had happened to him.

"I, I tried to stop the car on Main Street. The brakes gave out. Then I flipped," Hank whispered as he flashed back to the indistinct image of him crawling from the car, blood running down his face. He tried to sit up, but his head throbbed, and the room began to spin. Louise eased him back onto the bed.

"Baby, lay still now. The doctor says you'll need time. Easy, baby."

She carefully adjusted the pillow under Hank's head and then held his face with both of her hands. One tear rolled down Hank's face and she kissed it away gently.

"We're all here, baby." Hank relaxed. He looked to his left and saw his daughters for the first time.

"Hello there, my darlings."

"Hello daddy," they both said and leaned over to put their heads on their father's chest. He moved his left hand from one girl to the next, running his fingers through their hair.

The IV tugged at his arm again and he winced. He groaned and his daughters sat back up. He tried to smile. Slowly but surely, the medicine in the IV did its job. His eyes began to flutter and he was soon drifting away from his twin daughters. They cried gently in relief. Gallagher peeked his head back as he stepped into the room. Louise stood up from her chair and met Gallagher at the other side of the bed.

"Tell me more, Gallagher.'

"Well, like I said, your husband's crash was no accident. We checked the skid marks on the road where we think his car started to flip. He was traveling pretty fast, so we think he must have tried to regain control. The skid pattern showed how the tires lost contact with the road, but there was no braking pattern that suggested he hit the brakes before he flipped."

"And you have no doubts, Gallagher?"

"My people know their jobs, chief."

"Who would want my husband dead? It makes no sense."

"I don't have an answer for you, chief. But something stinks. If you don't mind, I'd like to help out if I can. During my free time, of course. I do have other crimes to solve and bad people to arrest. But when I can, I'll make myself available."

"That would be wonderful."

"Ok, well I'll let you be alone with your husband and your daughters. Give him my best when he comes around. I'll be in touch."

Gallagher shook Louise' hand and nodded at the twins. He stepped out of the room just as Mickey Cummings entered. They nodded at each other as Gallagher left.

Mickey's face was drawn. He looked at Hank as a monitor beeped next to Hank's bed. The IV bag was empty. A nurse came in and put a new bag on the metallic stand. She stepped out. Mickey stood at the foot of Hank's bed.

He knew Louise tolerated him, but Hank and Ken were Mickey's friends and teammates long ago. Well, he thought them friends, for his part anyway. There were too many times when they left him to fend for himself. Maybe if they had played that weekend, maybe if they had been with him that night on the Cape, he could have begged them to room with him. Inexplicably, they chose not to make the trip. They chose to let him go off alone that weekend. There was no turning back that calendar, no pulling back that dark thing. Still, he cared deeply for Ken and Hank.

"He ok?" Mickey moved closer to the bed.

The twins got up from their chairs and made room for him so he could stand close to their dad.

"He will be," Louise stepped closer to Mickey and drew him aside, opening the door and guiding him out into the hallway where nurses and doctors moved about. She looked down the hallway, like she thought someone might be listening. "It wasn't an accident, Mickey. Gallagher was just here and he said the brake lines had been cut."

"Christ."

"Something very bad is going on, Mickey."

Louise brought her hand to her mouth and trimmed the nail

to her left pinky finger.

"Do the girls know?"

"Yes."

"You're kidding me, right? They're just fifteen, Louise, for God's sake."

"They should know. They needed to know. I'm not protecting them, Mickey. There are too many people protecting others from the cruelty of the world. What haven't they seen already on the fucking internet?"

"But you're saying that someone tried to kill Hank. My God, Louise, do they need to know that?"

He stopped when Chief Consola's eyes blazed at him. He had crossed a line with her, one that no one crossed. He took a deep breath and held it for a moment before letting the air slowly escape. "I'm sorry." Mickey looked down the hallway and then back to Louise. His shoulders began to shake slightly. Louise took him by the arm and pulled him around the corner so no one would notice the mayor of Beaumont balling in a hospital corridor. She let him cry, finally moving closer and wrapping her arms around him. Mickey sobbed into Louise's chest. He was not a tall man, so his face rested against her breasts. In spite of outward appearances, when he had to be the mayor, he was a private man and he was ok with his emotions, as long as no one saw them. Beaumont was an evolved town, for the most part, but too much of what happened in Mickey's childhood couldn't be expressed to anyone, except maybe Louise, in this quiet, hidden and darker corner of the hospital. He pulled away and looked in her eyes. She held both of his hands and waited patiently for him to regain composure.

"This is how I run my family, Mick. It's been too difficult a week for you to be challenging me on this."

"I know. And I'm sorry. It's just there is so much going on right now and I can't make sense of it."

"Neither can I."

"Is there more to Ken's death than you've shared, Louise?"

"Yes, but I can't tell you now. I need to dig into it some more, and I will, now that the funeral is over and Hank is going to be ok."

"Do you think there's a connection between Hank's crash and Ken dying?"

"I'd be foolish to think otherwise. It's too much of a coincidence. Hank's accident just adds to the puzzle." She looked at him and then steered him farther away from the main hallway. "You've known Ken and Hank for years."

"I grew up with all of you. Played ball with Hank and Ken. You know that."

"But is there anything else that you know about them, or knew about them? Anything you can share?"

Mickey Cummings eyes moved almost imperceptibly. She noticed and cocked her head, opening the door for him to add more.

"Not really, no."

Mickey's eyes moved quickly, this time more distinctly. She also understood that he wasn't going to share anything at that moment, whatever it was. "I'd tell you if I could."

"Of course. I understand. I know this has been very difficult for you this week. You've done a good job holding the town together. Thank you so much for coming down, Mickey. I'll text you when Hank is doing better. Then maybe we can talk some more. I really need your help on this."

"Not many people say thank you for the work I do. Thank you for that, chief." Mickey started to walk away, but Louise took one of his hands and turned him back. She reached out and took his other hand. She looked at him intently, her eyes holding him in place.

"Mickey, I know your secret. I've always known. You've kept it to yourself, and I respect that. You don't need to, not from me."

"I'm sorry, but what secret is that?

"Too much is going on, and I'm not sure why I'm saying this now, but I know the secret you've kept."

"Do you?"

"I do. I don't think you need to keep that secret any longer. No one cares." He rubbed Louise' hands and looked at her like perhaps she couldn't understand the enormousness of his divulging the truth after so long, in a town like Beaumont.

"I don't agree. If I was going to come out, I should have done it years ago. But we all have our secrets, chief. Maybe I can do my job better if I keep my secret to who I am from our town."

"You don't have to hide it from anyone. It's 2019, for God's sake."

"Yes I do. I would have to sacrifice too much. Being gay isn't something the town will ever accept. Not being honest when I had the chance years ago is something I won't live down." He pulled her deeper into the corner of the hospital. "And I need you to respect my wish on this, Louise. I need to know you will not share this secret." A weariness came across his face.

"Of course I will respect your wishes. I would never do anything to embarrass you."

"Well, thank you for that. Too many times one thing leads to another. I hope you can understand."

"Mickey, what do you mean?"

"One thing leads to another, chief. Let's leave it alone, please."

She looked at him quizzically, as he took a deep breath and strode past her, down the hallway in front of the nurses' station. He pushed a large silver button that opened the door leading out of the ICU. He disappeared into a dense crowd of hospital personnel and walked away and even though he was the well-known and popular mayor of Beaumont, he was utterly and completely alone.

Louise watched him leave. Something else was going on with Mickey, but whatever it was, it would have to wait for another time for her to ask. She stepped back into her husband's room. The girls sat quietly as their mother joined them. She took their hands and the three of them bowed their heads and prayed together in the loneliness of Hank's room.

Chapter 12

A Long-Expected Call

The night had been long by the time Louise and the girls got back to their house from the hospital. Hank was stable and the doctors told them to go home.

She lay on her bed and stared up at the ceiling fan. It rotated slightly, moved around by the slight breeze blowing in from the open sliding door to the bedroom porch. It had been a restless night and there was no sleep for her. She rolled over and looked at Hank's side of the bed. Most of the covers had been pulled over to her side and Hank's pillows lay strewn on the floor.

She wondered why she admitted to Mickey that she knew he was gay, the same night as Hank's accident. She wasn't normally so impulsive, but the man looked so broken. Maybe her telling him made her feel better about all she had been through over the last week or so, like she needed to step outside herself and think of someone else. The mind works in strange ways. She wanted him to know that she knew and it was ok. Being gay didn't make Mickey slimy. He was that way all by himself. But perhaps she had comforted him in some way, just letting him know that she knew. Or maybe she fucked him up even more. She didn't know. She felt like she didn't understand anything, and just a week ago, she was worried about kids in town driving while using their cellphones or the occasional drunk at one of the local bars. Now she had Ken's death, her husband's crash and attempted murder, and blabbering to the mayor that she knew he was gay and agreeing to hold onto his secret. She took one of her pillows and flung it against the picture window in the bedroom. She took a couple of deep breaths and tried to put some of the pieces together.

Was there any hint that Ken was planning on killing himself? Had she or Hank missed something? The man had been over for a barbeque just a few days before he threw himself off the rope swing, and for the love of God, Louise only remembered that being a good day. Ken seemed quiet of course, because Ken was always quiet. Well, as she thought about it, lying on her bed, she thought he was more like he was contained, like he was holding tight to a darkness that threatened to spill out. When jokes were told, Ken would laugh like everyone, but not the belly laughing Hank and some of their other friends did that day. His laughs had been quiet, subdued and held back. Once Hank told her that Ken was like a hazy day; a shining sun that could not force its way through the mist.

Louise gave up the idea of sleep. She got up from her bed, pulled her robe closed, and went out on the porch. She had her cell phone with her and decided that even though it was four in the morning, she was going to call Jack Monroe. She wanted him to hear from her the news of Hank's crash. She looked in her contacts and found Jack's number. She punched some buttons and the dial tone began. After five or six rings, Jack answered the phone. His voice was groggy and coarse.

"Who is this?"

"Jack, it's Louise Consola. I know I woke you and I'm sorry. I thought you would like to hear from me about the news."

"What news?" Jack coughed to clear his voice.

"Hank's been in an accident."

"Dear God, what happened?"

"After the funeral, Hank went for a ride. His car was flipped downtown by the civil war statue. He's all busted up, Jack. He has a bad concussion and a broken arm, but he was lucky. The car exploded after Hank crawled away. He could have died, Jack."

"I'm so sorry, Louise. Is there something I can do? You know how I feel about your husband. It's been such a terrible week. First Ken, now Hank. My God."

"I didn't want you to find out through social media. I wanted you to hear it from me. Hank would have wanted that. I know it's been a difficult week for you, Jack. I know how much Hank and Ken meant to you. And Mickey Cummings. The mayor is devastated."

"I'm so sorry to hear that."

"Well, again, I'm sorry to wake you so early. I wanted to make sure you heard it from me."

"It's fine, Louise, and thank you for being so thoughtful."

"Of course. Goodbye."

Louise ended the call. She sat on a lounge chair, damp from the early morning dew, and waited for the light of the morning. She needed a good sunrise. She tightened her robe. First one tear formed, then another, and finally, Chief Louise Consola of the Beaumont Police Department cried out into the dim light of the morning.

Chapter 13

The One That Got Away

━━━━⋘◈⋙━━━━

Jack Monroe took his phone and walked out the door leading to the deck facing the woods in his backyard. The inground pool he had installed at the beginning of the summer was finally finished. The landscaping was perfect and the sod had grown in fully. The water shimmered as a lone flood light shined down on the aqua-marine surface. He looked down at the phone and swiped until he came to the link to the Boston Globe. He looked at the article about the accident in Beaumont where the husband of the chief of police had been in a car crash. He had seen the article on the Globe online service hours ago. Louise' call had been expected, really for hours, and Jack grinned that it had taken so long for her to contact him. Of course, she would contact him. So kind and considerate. Stupid, obtuse woman.

Jack stood on his deck and watched the light of the morning start to overwhelm the evening gloom. It was unfortunate that Hank survived the crash. Not all of Jack's plans came to fruition. He knew that Hank would lose it after Ken's funeral. That's why he stole into Hank's garage. It was dumb luck that they took Louise' car to the funeral. And lovely Beaumont, so trusting, no one ever locks their doors or even keeps their garage shut. Park down the street, just walk in, cut the wires, just enough so they would snap eventually, and off Jack skulked. Most of the neighborhood was at the funeral, so there were no eyes to notice his furtive movements.

Fucking Hank Consola. Jack had thought once, years ago, that Hank might have been an easy mark, but that proved false. That was one boy he knew he had to leave alone, at least at the time. Why put in all that effort when there were others so malleable?

Jack's hand squeezed his phone as his anger began to rise. His hairy knuckles held it firm against his thigh. He had tried once more with Hank, such a beautiful boy, such a fine, glittering prize. It was a phone call he made to Hank's dad. Jack's little league team, the Red Sox, had won Beaumont's American League, Little League championship, again. One of the perks of winning was that Jack could add three minor league players to his roster. Doing so guaranteed that those three boys would automatically be placed on Jack's team the following season. Jack had crafted the rule himself. The rest of the league's governing board had gone along. Silly, ignorant men, agreeing to a rule that would benefit him at the expense of the kids. Winning.

So Jack made three calls, one to Hank, one to Mickey Cummings, and one more to Ken Richardson. Mickey and Ken said yes, right away. They were overwhelmed at the idea that they were being picked to play in the town championship against the Cardinals from the National League, the other league in town from the east side of the tracks. And by the legendary coach Jack Monroe. But Hank said no. He claimed he wanted to finish out the season with his minor league team. He said he didn't want to leave his team in the lurch. Silly boy. Still, Jack got Ken and Mickey.

But Hank said no, and now Ken was dead. Seeing the pictures of Ken's bloated, pecked-at body ruined the memory of Ken's long, sinewy legs, his fine black hair, his deep, full lips. It had been easy, Jack thought to himself. Just enough burgers and fries, trips to Williamsport and the Cape, sitting with him and the rest of the team at one of the many movies Jack paid for, his leg resting slightly against Ken's. It was dark so no one could see the thickness under Jack's khakis.

Jack was a hometown hero now. But Ken's death ruined it. Why did the boy have to off himself on Jack's day? The attention of the town was turned away from Jack as the news of Ken's death spread. He had earned his day, with all he had done for the boys. It was always about the boys.

He checked his phone again. His next trip to Williamsport was less than a week away. He checked the roster; fifteen boys, all paid up by their parents, only one other chaperone. They would stay in a hotel not far from the baseball fields, set back away from the highway, hidden perfectly by a young stand of trees.

Jack's mind raced. How might anyone connect him to Ken's death? Hank of course, so maybe there would be another chance to take him down. And then there was Mickey Cummings. Sweet little Mickey Cummings, but he had kept quiet so far. Jack had the video, so Mickey wouldn't squeal. He sat by his pool and delighted in that fact as a lovely sunrise spread across Beaumont.

"Here, have some of my popcorn, Ken." Jack handed over the oversized tub. Ken dug his small hands into the bucket. Jack took back the tub. He placed his hand on Ken's leg, deliberately, then took it off quickly. "There's more, if you want some," a double entendre. The movie played on the screen. Jack's other hand worked, clandestine in the dark.

Chapter 14

Gallagher

Louise sat in her office. Hank had been out of the hospital for a few days and was doing well, physically. His silence was expected. His best friend was dead and buried and he had come close to losing his family, so of course, his silence wasn't a surprise. Louise gave him the space she thought he needed. They would talk more in time, she knew.

Gallagher sat across from Louise. He sat tall in his chair. Betty stood against the door, arms folded. She was in her civilian clothes. It was her day off, but she stopped by Louise' office anyway. She knew her boss might need the support. The police station hummed as different officers ended their shifts and others came on duty.

"Tell me more about the clothes you found, chief." Gallagher spoke in his monotone rumble.

"Running outfit and a kid's pair of gold, Converse All-Stars. Ken tied them tightly and tossed them into the crater left behind by the root ball."

Betty shifted her position against the door. "Same shoes that Hank wore when he and Ken played ball when they were kids?" she asked.

"Yes. Same shoes."

"Any thoughts about that?" Gallaher looked intently into

Louise' eyes.

"Ken clearly had a reason to add his hoop shoes to the bundle."

"Probably," Gallagher took in a deep breath and let it out slowly. "Who else was on Ken's team, aside from your husband?"

"Mickey played on that team," Betty added. She moved toward the desk and pulled up another chair.

"Yes, he did." Louise leaned forward and rested her elbows on her desk. Her service gun sat on the corner. It gleamed metallic blue from the light streaming through the window. The three of them sat quietly, pondering the questions that haunted them. Finally, Louise broke the silence.

"Betty, could you please go down the hall and ask the mayor to come in?" Betty got up and opened the door and disappeared down the hallway. In a moment, Mickey Cummings stepped in. He held a thin, unlit cigar in his mouth. Betty walked in behind him and shut the door. Mickey took Betty's chair. Gallagher stood up and reached his hand out to Mickey. Mickey stood back up and took the cigar out of his mouth. They shook hands awkwardly. Gallagher sat back down and turned in his chair to face Mickey. Betty returned to her spot against the door. She crossed her arms over her chest and waited.

"I'm glad Hank is home and doing better, Louise," Mickey sighed as Gallagher looked on.

"Mickey, we found some clothes tied up not far from the rope swing. They were thrown into the bottom of that big,

81

overturned oak. You remember that tree?"

Mickey leaned back in his chair. Louise could see Mickey's jaw work on the cigar. His facial muscles flexed and relaxed.

"I remember that tree. It's not far from the rope swing." His eyes looked off at a piece of art on Louise' wall. "We spent a lot of time there when we were kids. That hurricane we had years ago knocked that tree down, if I remember, when we were kids. Weird. It was the strongest tree around. We used to climb it every day."

"We found these, Mickey."

Louise opened up a drawer in her desk and pulled out a large plastic bag. She undid the twist tie that held it closed and pulled out the gold Converse All-Stars. She placed them carefully on her desk, like something about them was sacred. She turned them slightly so Mickey could clearly see the white "All-Star" emblem festooned on both ankles. The shoes looked old and the soles were almost devoid of tread. The toes were stained black from all the time Ken wore them playing in the forest by the river. They were made mostly from canvas, long since abandoned as the chief material of hoop shoes. Now they were made of synthetic material, probably from Vietnam or China. You couldn't buy them today for under a hundred bucks. Back in the day, they cost one-tenth the price and lasted twice as long. Old things were like that; they lasted forever.

Mickey reached over.

"May I?"

"Of course."

He took hold of both shoes. He sat back in his chair and

examined them, like he was looking at an old photo from his youth. He turned them in his hands and rubbed his fingers along the worn-out treads. He touched the laces that had been broken and retied many times. No one spoke. The light from the window darkened as a cloud moved across the sky. A commuter bus moved along Main Street. It's diesel engine belched smoke and the noise made an almost imperceptible vibration in the office. Finally, he sat back up and carefully placed the hoop shoes back on Louise' desk in exactly the same place where she had placed them moments before.

"I had shoes just like these." Mickey looked over at Gallagher. "Everyone on the team did."

"Were you a close team, Mickey?" Gallagher asked as Louise sat back in her chair.

"As close as any team, I suppose, but Hank and Ken were inseparable. I was a bit jealous, to be honest." Mickey began to work on his cigar again. He bit down and worked at it from one side of his mouth to the other. Gallagher noticed. Betty remained silent, leaning with her arms crossed over her chest, trying to catch the nuance of the conversation. She reached up and scratched an itch just below her eye.

"Tell us more," Gallaher said. Mickey shifted in his chair and took the cigar out of his mouth.

"The only time they weren't on the same team was when Jack picked the three of us to play on the Red Sox in the playoffs when we were nine. Ken was thrilled to be asked, but Hank turned it down. I always wondered about that."

"Why did Hank turn it down, Mickey?" Louise sat back up, straight in her chair. She folded her hands and placed them on her desk.

"He said he didn't want to desert his minor league team during their playoffs."

"But you guys were ok leaving your minor league team?" Gallagher asked.

"Well, Ken and my teams were not in the playoffs." Mickey spoke like his memory of being nine was perfect.

"So the two of you joined the Red Sox. Who was the coach?

"Jack Monroe was our coach."

"Jack Monroe, the hometown hero?" Gallagher looked quizzically at Mickey.

"Yes," Mickey felt his stomach tighten. He was treading in a dark place and he was unsure where it might lead. A roll of skin furrowed on his forehead, just below the edge of his wavy, white hair. "Why?" he asked a bit defensively.

"No reason, mayor. I'm sure he's broken up about all of this as much as you."

Gallagher shifted his weight slightly in his chair. Mickey sat quietly, trying to avoid going down a darker path. He crossed one leg over the other and tried to control his breathing.

"I'm going to Jack's house this afternoon, Mickey. I'd like to talk with him about his teams and these shoes. Do you want to come with me?" Louise asked.

Mickey's eyes flickered for the briefest moment. Louise and

Gallagher caught the movement before Mickey could control it. They looked at each other quickly and then turned back to Mickey.

"Would you mind if I pass? I'm so goddamn busy right now."

Louise noticed Mickey bit down a bit harder on his cigar.

"That's fine. No worries. I understand how busy you are." Mickey got up and shook Gallagher's hand. He walked toward the door that Betty had opened for him. Betty put her hand gently on Mickey's shoulder as he walked down the hall to his office. He stepped in quickly and shut the door quietly behind him. Betty came back in. Louise' office remained silent for a few moments as all three of them absorbed all that Mickey had to say.

"That was strange," Gallagher sat back down in the same chair Mickey had sat in moments before.

It was very warm, with a hint of moisture from Mickey's backside. Gallagher noticed and got up quickly. He sat back down in the other chair.

"He knows something," Gallagher said.

Louise looked at him for a bit.

"Chief, the mayor is holding something back."

"He did seem nervous."

"I'm not sure about your mayor. What's your take on him?"

Louise moved some hair away from her face. She took the length of her hair in her right hand and adjusted the elastic that kept it in place. Gallagher sat patiently.

"Mickey's good. Slimy sometimes, but he's a good man. Does a nice job with the town, although he could ease up on always running for office."

"His eyes danced when I asked him about Jack Monroe."

Gallagher and Louise looked at each other. He pursed his mouth slightly, like he was thinking something through.

"Tell me more about him."

Louise sat in her chair and looked across her office. She could hear the hum of the station as different officers went about their business, taking calls or filling out paperwork; the normal, monotonous day in the life of a police station in a quiet, unblemished town. She thought of Hank at home, on the couch probably, his arm still in its cast and his head healing slowly. She thought of Ken's funeral and the kind words of solace offered by different friends and family. And she thought of Mickey Cummings trying to hold the town together while he kept his secret; one that she knew he didn't need to keep. She was sure of it. The town would accept Mickey being gay. It was 2019, for Christ's sake. Still, she knew she would keep his secret, like hiding a baby cub in the woods from a pack of wolves. Mickey thought it needed to be kept a secret. So that's what she would do; keep Mickey's hidden life secret, for his sake. They had grown up together and that was worth something. Probably worth quite a bit.

"Mickey is the mayor. He grew up here and cares about the place. He's always there to help out or shake a hand. And he's always done things for others without letting on that he did them. I've seen little things. He's gone shopping, early in the morning and when no one was around to see him do it, and he's collected the grocery carts and herded them back to the store. I've heard that he would buy gift cards and drop them off quietly in someone's mailbox, maybe a person down on her or his luck. No name on the card, just Mickey buying twenty bucks of groceries or a game card for a kid who got in trouble at school. Yeah, he's always looking for another vote, but that's part of the job. It's the slimy part of Mickey everyone sees. It's not what I see though. It's like he's a painting where you get drawn in by the fancy colors, but you need only take a deeper look and see the tiny details."

She turned back at Gallagher.

"Seems like a good man, all in all."

"He is."

She took hold of the basketball sneakers and put them back in their bag. She leaned down and picked up her backpack that sat on the floor next to her desk. She unzipped it and placed the basketball shoes at the bottom. She stood up quickly and slung the backpack over her shoulder.

"Do you want to drive out with me to Jack Monroe's place, Gallagher?"

She reached over her desk and carefully picked up her handgun, fastening it carefully onto the holster on her right hip.

"Do you mind? I would like to meet Jack Monroe. Something's odd about all of this."

"What are you thinking about?"

"I'm not sure, but he's the only connection. He was their

coach. And it seems odd to me that only Hank declined Jack's offer to join his team back when your husband played little league. Why not join the majors and play in the town championship? And play for the legend of Jack Monroe? Why would Ken and the mayor agree and Hank say no? It's the town championship. Maybe your hometown hero can help us understand why Ken and the mayor said yes and Hank said no. So I'm coming with you."

"I think I'd like to get your perspective on whatever Jack can share to help us out, so that would be good, Gallagher."

Louise held the door for him. The two of them walked out of the office and left the building. They got into Louise' SUV with the blue and gold "Beaumont" lettering and the white "Protecting All of Our Community" stenciled on the driver's side door. She drove out of the parking lot and down main street.

She was sure Jack Monroe could use the support right about now. It must be very hard, knowing that one of his boys killed himself and another one badly hurt in a car crash.

Gallagher sat in the passenger's seat, anxious to meet Jack Monroe, the legend. He rubbed the bridge of his nose with his meaty hand and watched the unblemished beauty of Beaumont roll by.

The four of them played pickup at the park down by Pomp's pond. Mickey and Hank on one team; Jack and Ken on the other. Ken stole the ball from Mickey and drove to the basket. He laid the ball up perfectly. The sound of the chain-link netting crackled

as the ball dropped through. He ran back on defense. Jack gave him a tap on the backside as Ken picked up Mickey once again. Ken beamed from his coach's encouragement. He set up in a defensive stance, intent on stealing the ball again. A coach's encouragement goes a long way.

Chapter 15

Hoop Shoes

———— ❦ ————

Jack sat on a chair at his kitchen table. His laptop was open and once again, he went through the roster of his boys. He flipped through the data and stared at each boy's picture. Good boys. Strong boys. His team had lost to the Giants in the town championship just a few weeks earlier. He consoled them as only he could, he thought to himself. Two of the boys on the team didn't get into any of the games. It was too bad for them, because Jack only played the very best. He was nothing if not a winner. Those two had pleaded for more playing time. They wanted to get into the game so badly. One had cried when the series was over because he never got off the bench. Tommy Timmons. Sweet, lovely, Tommy Timmons, the youngest player on the team. He didn't have many friends, although the rest of the boys liked him just fine. He was worried about who would be his roommate on the trip. Jack would make sure Tommy would not bunk alone. After all, the boy did want more playing time.

It really hadn't been too difficult, the grooming. Just find someone a bit needy, a bit lonely, maybe someone from a family with something amiss, a broken home perhaps, or an absentee father, or a hurting mother, a family with a chink in the armor. Towns like Beaumont had plenty of boys just like that if you just took the time to look carefully. Most families were ashamed when things didn't look perfect. Everything had to look perfect, especially for the parents, and that's where Jack could help out the most.

And of course, there was the sports. How many families worshipped at the altar of the scholarship? Just how wonderful was it for a mother or father to brag about their kid, the one who made it, the one with the scholarship to play basketball or baseball or soccer, hockey or football or lacrosse? The bragging was the thing for the parents, he noticed, and if he could sell them the myth of it all, gain access to the little boys, the pickings would be easy. How many parents had been willing to ignore the truth, just hold on to the irrationality of the myth of the scholarship, and put their trust in the man who guaranteed access to coveted exposure and elite tournaments, trips to the Cape or access to premiere teams. He was the gatekeeper, opening and closing doors as he saw fit. He had the power of it, and he wielded it discriminately. Most of the boys never saw it coming until they were in too deep and the shame and humiliation became the engine of their silence. What a wonderful, wonderful world.

Jack looked up from his keyboard. A tremor of anxiety took hold of him as he watched a Beaumont Police Department cruiser coming down his long driveway. Both doors opened and Chief Louise Consola and another man stepped out. They stepped onto his porch and knocked on his door. He froze with his fingers on the keyboard. He shook out of his paralysis, making sure to minimize the tabs with the pictures of his boys before he slammed the laptop shut. Tommy's picture was the last to be clicked off.

Jack got up from his chair and walked over to the door. He

adjusted his glasses, checking his reflection in a mirror that hung against the wall by the door. He noticed a slight fog on his glasses. He took his flannel shirt and wiped it away. Placing his glasses back on the bridge of his nose, he tightened the elastic band, pulling the frames hard against his face. Gathering himself, he opened the front door slowly. It was the chief of police.

"Hello Jack. Do you mind if we come in?"

"Of course, please chief."

Jack stood out of the way to make room for Louise to enter, followed by the stranger. Jack noticed the man wore a blue state police uniform.

"Jack, this is Mike Gallagher, state police."

"Hello, officer Gallagher. Come in please. Can I get you some coffee?"

Jack led them into the kitchen. Books and papers were strewn about, mostly books on youth sports, interspersed with sports pages with headlines of Jack's many championships. Gallagher picked up one of the newspapers and read the headline.

"Tough loss, Jack." He held the paper up. The headline said, "Giants Top Red Sox for Little League Championship." Jack turned quickly to face Gallagher. A flash of anger passed across Jack's face. His jaw clenched and his dark eyebrows furrowed. Just as quickly, his face morphed back to affected calm, with Jack's mouth turning into a grin, kind of like the expression a kid would make if he had just been found out screwing over one of his buddies.

"Yeah, that was a tough one. But my boys played great." He took his laptop and unplugged it, zipping it up in a black laptop carrier. He walked past Gallagher and over to where Louise was standing. She gazed out of Jack's kitchen window to the new pool in his backyard and the forest that surrounded Jack's house. Shadows began to stretch out towards the porch, extending long, dark fingers up to the place where Jack normally sat. He reached up and stuffed his laptop in a cabinet by the refrigerator. Pictures of his teams adorned his refrigerator door, hung there with reliable magnets

"Nice pool, Jack."

"I thought I'd splurge on myself, just this once."

"Well, of course you deserve it," she said as she found herself a chair.

Jack took three mugs from a cabinet and filled them with coffee. He set them down in front of Louise and Gallagher. Jack took a seat with his back to the porch and the pool and the dark forest.

"I wanted to make sure you were ok, Jack. I didn't see you at Ken's funeral."

Louise took a small sip from her coffee. It was bitter and she put it down, careful not to show any sign that it tasted bad.

"I'm fine, and thanks for coming by. This might sound awful, but the timing of all of this is terrible. I've got a trip to Williamsport coming up. I still have so much to do."

"Yes, it must be terrible," Gallagher spoke slowly.

Jack looked at him quickly and then turned back to Louise. She held her cup in both hands but did not take another sip.

"Is there some way I can help, chief?"

He uncrossed his left leg and replaced it with his right. His foot bobbed up and down like he had something else to do and was waiting impatiently for his guests to get on with things.

"Do you recognize these shoes?" Louise pulled the blue and gold Converse All-Stars out from her backpack and placed them on Jack's kitchen table. Jack put his coffee down and stared at the shoes. Gallagher sat silently, watching Jack intently. Jack looked at the shoes for a few seconds.

"Should I?"

He crossed his arms over his chest and looked from Gallagher to Louise.

"These were the shoes Ken, Hank, and Mickey Cummings wore when they played basketball on your team."

"Well, yes, of course. Now I remember. That entire team had to have the same shoes. I think they all purchased them together."

Louise sat silently, waiting for Jack to go on. Gallagher remained quiet. He took a small sip from his mug and put it down carefully.

"I found them tied up not far from where Ken was found. We think he placed them in the crater at the big overturned oak tree on the hill overlooking the river. His running clothes were with them, so it had to be Ken's shoes."

Jack looked at the shoes. He reached over to pick them up, but then his hand drew back, almost like the shoes were too hot to touch. He folded his arms instead and sat up straight in his chair. His expression was blank but his eyes moved back and forth between Louise and Gallagher.

"That's odd. Why would Ken do that?"

Gallagher took another sip from his mug. He put it down and leaned forward. He put both of his large hands on the kitchen table.

"Chief Consola and I are stumped and we thought since you were so close to the boys, you might be able to share something with us, anything really, so we can maybe understand why Ken did what he did."

Gallagher folded his hands and waited.

"I don't know what to say about this. It ended up being a terrible day. You know I was honored as a home-town hero the same day they found Ken's body. I was a yo-yo. It was just terrible."

Jack took another sip from his mug and crossed his legs, for the third time. Again, his foot continued to bob up and down.

"I'm sorry, but I'm not sure how I can help. It's still such a bloody shame."

Gallagher wondered if Jack was referring to Ken's death or Jack's day being ruined.

Louise and Gallagher sat motionless. They never took their

eyes off of Jack. The speed that his foot bobbed about increased just enough that it registered with Louise and Gallagher who looked at each other quickly. Gallagher rubbed his chin slowly and Louise took a quiet breath. They held his gaze until Louise clapped her hands once, ending their conversation. She turned to Gallagher and then back to Jack.

"Ok, Well, thank you Jack. I know you're busy so we'll let you get back to finalizing your trip to Williamsport. Let's go, Gallagher."

Louise stood up and shook Jack's hand. Gallagher got up as well and extended his long arm. He shook hands with Jack and held the grip for a few seconds and held Jack's gaze before finally disengaging. They both walked out of Jack's kitchen. Jack moved along behind them. They opened the front door and walked to the cruiser. Louise started up the engine and backed out of the long driveway, through the forest now fully enveloped in shadow. She put the car in drive and drove off, disappearing as she headed back to the station. It was silent around Jack's house as he watched them drive off. He closed the door, careful not to make any sound and retreated back through his house and out the door to his back porch. He sat in his lawn chair and looked out over his shimmering pool. He pulled his phone out and swiped it until he found the Instagram of Ken's body, pecked at by birds, rotting in the afternoon sun.

He thought about the visit and the basketball shoes the chief had shown him. Those glorious, perfect, basketball shoes. How well they fit his boys, their sublime feet fitting snugly within. And they wore them everywhere, so much so that they didn't know where their feet ended and the golden shoes began. But Louise had brought them to his house. Why? Maybe Hank had said something, or Mickey Cummings. Jack sat quietly, peering off into the gloom. All he had achieved was now being ruined by the death of Ken Richardson and his failure trying to get rid of Hank. And then there was Mickey Cummings. Sweet, easy Mickey Cummings.

Jack sat and thought some more about how it might all be taken away by Hank and Mickey. He had no intention of letting all he had succeeded in doing be stripped away. He seethed as he looked out over his backyard, the master of his domain. He removed his glasses and rubbed his nose with a hairy thumb and forefinger. He set his glasses back in place. He looked down again at the Instagram image of Ken's dead body. He ground his teeth and made two fists which he pounded against his legs. His phone slipped from his grasp and landed at his feet. He swung his leg like he was going to kick it but somehow controlled at least that dark impulse. His backyard became very dark, a lone light shining down behind him, illuminating the depth of his pool.

Fenway Park was crowded, of course. But it was just the two of them, this time. Hank had said no, that his parents needed him home that night. Not a problem.

Ken swallowed the last of his hot dog. Mustard crusted the corner of his mouth and his fingers were sticky from the soda he had spilled when a foul ball came their way. Jack had reached out and grabbed it from another boy, one row in front, when the silly kid bobbled it. Jack held the ball high above his head and basked in the applause. It grew louder when he handed the ball to Ken. What a wonderful gesture, they all thought. Ken beamed as he held the ball in his precious hands, looking up in admiration to the man who was becoming so important to him. It didn't matter that his coach stole the ball from the little boy in the row in front of them.

Chapter 16

The Forest from the Trees

Louise and Gallagher sat in a booth at Morton's Deli on Main Street. Gallagher ate a glazed donut and sipped some coffee, the kind he preferred rather than the swill Jack had served him. Louise ate a cruller and swallowed some orange juice. They ate and drank for a bit before either of them spoke, thinking about their visit with Jack Monroe. Other customers ate late lunches and sipped strong coffee. Cars drove silently down Main Street, their engines muffled by the thick glass of the deli. No one paid attention to Louise and Gallagher. Pedestrians walked by on Main street and went about their business. A thin rain began to fall and the pedestrians quickened their pace.

"Something very odd about Jack Monroe, chief. His eyes danced when you questioned him about the basketball shoes. He wouldn't even touch them."

"I think he's still shaken by everything. Ken and Hank and the rest of his boys meant so much to him."

"And he's always been a youth sports coach?"

"As long as I've known him and Hank and Ken."

"What's that, twenty years? Doesn't that seem odd?"

"What are you getting at, Gallagher?"

"Just seems peculiar to me, that's all."

"He has no family, Gallagher. I think it is wonderful that he's dedicated his entire life to those boys." Gallagher took a long drink from his coffee mug. He set it down gently and placed his massive hands flat on the table. He looked at Louise, letting the innuendo take effect.

"Christ, Gallagher. The town just made him a home-town hero."

"That adds to the oddity. Look, you have to admit that the timing of everything is way off. You have a parade for Jack and Ken's body is found on the dam the very same day. Back in my academy days, we might have called that a clue." Gallaher folded his hands. "Think about what he said in the video. He said he'd carried something for too long and it had become too much. And then we find his fucking basketball sneakers in the crater near the root ball. He was leaving a clue, chief."

"I know, but what might that have to do with Jack Monroe? He loved those boys."

"Hmm," Gallagher grunted and finished the remaining coffee from his mug. He stood as he opened his wallet and pulled out enough money for the bill and the tip. "Call me if you need me, but step back and think about it, chief. It's possible you are too close to this. This thing stinks."

He walked out the door and down Main Street to where he had left his car not far from the police station. Louise sat and looked at the tip, instinctively, like she always did when she, Hank, and the girls had dinner together. She looked out at the cars driving by and the people going here and there in the rain. This was a wonderful town, her town, perfect in its uniqueness and suburban bliss and she did not wish to go down the dark path Gallagher seemed to be hinting at. There had to be something about giving a townie the benefit of the doubt.

She thought back to the day of Jack's ceremony. She watched as countless men stood and applauded when Mickey Cummings gave Jack the key to the city, former players all. She thought of Jack in the same way; a hero and someone who had dedicated his life to the town and to youth sports and she was reluctant to think otherwise. Something stunk about what was going on, but she was reluctant to admit to Gallagher's suggestion that somehow Jack Monroe was involved.

She sat by herself and thought about how her girls were in high school now and she had to admit that she was glad that the youth sports beast had been left behind. She had always felt that Beaumont, shit, the rest of the country had made youth sports into a religion. How many times had she and the girls missed church because they had a Sunday travel soccer game or some other "elite" competition? Elite. How could some twelve-year-old girl or boy be considered elite? How could some adult think they would be able to make a decision about kids before they had even had the chance to reach puberty, yet there she and Hank were, dutifully pacing the sidelines as the girls played on the soccer pitch or whacked other parent's kids with lacrosse sticks.

She and Hank had been more balanced in their views of their daughters, knowing that they were good athletes, like most of the other kids, but not great, like almost all of the other kids, but still, it was tough to ignore it when other parents bragged about paying private coaches for specialized instruction or when they signed up their precious daughters or son's for elite summer camps. Hell, most of their friends had kids who played the same sport year-round. And the coaches.

Few in town had more political clout than the elite team coaches, who could decide on a whim whether someone was going to play and be a star, or even get a chance to gain access to the coveted high school sport's pipeline. Christ, people in town worshipped these youth coaches, or got them fired, if it suited their need. Somehow, Jack Monroe had kept his coaching positions in baseball and basketball for years, probably because he never asked for any money. Almost all of the youth coaches got paid these days. Maybe it was easier to justify getting rid of someone when you had a say in their pay. Hell, most youth coaches got paid more than high school coaches. In America, that is how you are judged, by the money you get paid, even if it was youth sports. Doing it for nothing had made Jack Monroe insulated from the carnage. Maybe he understood that all along.

Decades later and he was still in the dugout or on the bench. And it didn't seem like there was anytime soon when he would give up coaching. So many more boys to coach. But parents got too close to all of it. Louise and Hank had been chewed on by the jaws of the sports beast. Maybe Gallagher was right? Maybe she and Hank were too close to see the situation clearly, like it was the glass of a lighthouse that needed way more cleaning than it could get, and it blinded you if you looked too closely. Maybe the lighthouse was too bright and Louise couldn't see the beams from the light. She checked herself and admitted that maybe she was too close to all of this to see clearly.

She left the diner and walked back to her office at town hall. She stepped in briefly to see if anyone was still around. It was just the nighttime crew. Mickey Cumming's office was dark. She checked her desk and straightened it up a bit. She couldn't leave a day's worth of paperwork on her desk until the next day, so she finished it up. She was diligent that way. Something always came up to mess with her schedule. She finished her work and turned her light off. She walked out of her office and closed the door. Betty was sitting at her desk, checking her cell phone for any news bulletins.

"Christ, go home Betty."

"You too, chief," and with that, Louise Consola left the building and got in her cruiser. She left the parking lot and drove home. She hoped Hank was still up. Something about the way Gallagher had talked with her about Jack Monroe gnawed at her, and their visit out to his place certainly was strange, she had to admit. There were things she needed to ask her husband about his days playing baseball and basketball under the tutelage of coach Jack Monroe. She just wanted to find the right time. Her husband was still in pain. She needed to be especially sensitive to how she broached the subject. All these thoughts coursed through her mind as he drove out toward their house, the intensifying rain pounding down on Beaumont.

"You know, I'm not trying to be your father. You already have one, even if he's away on business like he is so often. You must miss him very much. You know you can always count on me for

anything, Ken. Anything. Jack put his hand on the headrest on Ken's seat. It was just the two of them, this time, after a Celtic's game, in the parking lot of the warehouse across from McDonald's. They shared a bag of burgers and fries. Two almost empty drink containers sat between their legs. "Maybe next weekend we can go fishing. Would you like that? I know just the place."

Chapter 17

A Dark Thing

Hank Consola sat on the couch in the living room. The girls had gone off to bed. He had reminded them to leave their cell phones on the kitchen table. Their two smartphones sat stacked, recharging.

His arm still ached. His cracked skull felt better, although there was still an occasional dizzy spell. He fidgeted on the couch. He thought about taking some more of the pain meds the doctor had prescribed. That would be one way to put his mind at ease, at least in the temporary way he needed. Almost two weeks from Ken's suicide and his mind remained tormented. He didn't see a way clear of the thoughts swirling through his head. The pain meds would help, but he thought better of it, perhaps a mistake.

He sat in the dark, waiting for his wife to come home. He wondered if there was a statute of limitations on the promises people make when they're little. What's the price for keeping a promise, especially when your best friend lay draped over a concrete dam? Do you ever get forgiven for holding onto a secret until you have to throw dirt on a person's casket? Hank began to sweat as these horrible thoughts forced their way through the barriers he had erected so carefully and deliberately. Now, broken and weakened by the events of the last two weeks, his mind could not hold back the dirty river of thoughts that coursed desperately toward the waterfall of endless shame. It terrorized him to even acknowledge that he might not be able to hold back the flow. He leaned back and looked up at the ceiling and a piece of him wished the entire house would collapse on his head.

Louise pulled her cruiser into the garage. She stepped through the door and put her keys to the cruiser down on the kitchen table. She unbuckled her holster and carefully placed her gun on the table. She pulled out a key from her pocket and opened a safe that sat under the kitchen table. She turned the key and an electric code came up on the screen. She punched in a set of numbers and the safe popped open. She placed her gun and holster inside the safe next to another hand gun she and Hank kept for when Louise was out of the house. She undid the top two buttons to her uniform and stepped over to Hank. She sat down close to her husband, placing her hand on his leg. Normally, those two gestures would be enough to get Hank interested, but tonight, she knew it wasn't the right time to horse around with her husband. Shit, he had barely spoken since the crash, never mind since Ken's death. She kissed him gently on the cheek and rested her head on his shoulder. They both sank into the couch. It had been another long day.

"You good?" She looked up at Hank.

"Some."

He grew quiet again. Louise reached up and turned off the light to the living room. The house grew dark except for a nightlight that glowed near the safe. They could hear coyotes argue off in the distance. A skunk had been by not too long ago.

"Well, that smells lovely."

She laughed in the darkness.

"I hadn't really noticed," he murmured.

She sat quietly for a bit.

"Would you like to talk?"

"I'm very tired."

"You haven't said much since the funeral or the accident."

"I still have a lot to sort out."

"Do tell."

She nestled in a bit closer.

"Not yet," he sighed.

Louise nudged him a bit and turned to look at her husband.

"It's ok. When you're ready. Take your time, baby. Whatever you have to say can wait another day."

"Can it? There's another trip in a couple of days."

"Wait, what are you talking about?" Louise reached her hand out, placing it carefully against his face.

She looked at her husband. A sliver of fear began to form in her. He sat there and didn't move. A paralysis extended from his face down his torso. HIs legs stuck out straight and he didn't move.

"Come, let's go upstairs, Hank. We can talk up there or you can just hold me. We haven't held each other in a while. Come on baby."

She smiled encouragingly and waited for Hank to take her

hand. He sat quietly in the dark and did not move.

"You go up. I'm going to sit here for a while."

He looked off toward the safe where two guns waited. Louise felt a small tremor course through her body. As a police officer, she felt an odd vibration, the kind she might feel when talking a perp away from doing something stupid. As Hank's wife, the vibration was deeper, primal in the darkness, like she was trying to see without light, staring at the man who sat in shadow.

"Come up when you can, then. Do you want me to turn on a light?"

"No. Just let me sit in the dark."

He looked up to the space his wife left behind when she walked upstairs. It was like she was disappearing, no longer a part of his consciousness.

Hank stared off into the darkness of his living room. It had been close, the letting out. He wanted desperately to reveal the dark thing he held deep inside, but it still caged his mind, a familiar beast struggling to form and worm its way out. Hank wasn't sure how much longer he could contain the animal. But there was another trip in a few days. Another one of Jack's trips.

He felt the animal rip and slash at his mind, tearing it, bleeding it out. With an immense effort, he barely regained control of the creature. He pushed it back, but not as far this time. It was like another long, rolling tide that gained on the contours of the beach, moving relentlessly before it overcame the sandcastles of his mind. His body sagged and slowly, his eyelids began to droop. Finally, he felt himself pass off to a place where he hoped his mind could rest. Instead, he dreamed of the beast with its long, dark claws grasping at him appallingly from the depths of a black, bottomless pond. The beast held him down, but cruelly allowed him to see from where he floated, deep under the pond, a lone rope swing close to a cavernous root ball crater and an enormous, dead oak laying across broken trees. The beast flung Hank over the edge and down into the crater. He tried to scream and climb out, but clawing fingers from the roots held him down and his voice was lost in the blackness. He tried to bellow for help, but the dead tree and its roots pulled him deeper into the unyielding earth, muffling all sounds and enveloping him in utter darkness.

Finally, the roots overwhelmed him. He was dragged deeper into the pit, lit now from below by a consuming fire. Images crawled toward him, small boys broken and disfigured. They grabbed onto his legs, biting down fiercely with rotted jaws. He struck at them with his hands and feet but they would not release him from their hateful bites. The nightmare continued until finally, the boys released their jaws and swam away. A different boy, familiar to Hank, reached out with gnarled hands and bit into his face. He shook Hank like a dog shakes a cat it intends to kill. Hank struggled to get free, but the boy's jaws tightened, and his hands pulled Hank closer until he could see clearly the face of Ken Richardson. His head was fractured and contorted, one eye missing from his skull. His ribs stuck out from his rotting flesh and parts of his thighs were missing like something evil had feasted on its dark meat. He screamed at Hank, a wail of dark anguish.

"You should have been with me, you should have been with

me!"

Ken's face contorted into an oval scream. Finally, Hank kicked out and Ken's boyish, broken form fell back, deep into the pit until he disappeared in the fire. Hank felt himself pulled toward the fire, its flames searing him until just before he was consumed, he willed himself back into consciousness like you can do sometimes when a dream threatens to destroy you.

He stood suddenly, frightened to his core. He strained to regain control of himself, forcing the black dream back into the cave of his unconsciousness. Finally, barely, using what remained of his strength, he regained control of his tortured reality. He used his good hand to work his way out of the kitchen, stubbing his toes twice along the way. He reached out and found the stairs leading up to his bedroom. Slowly, excruciatingly, he willed himself up the stairs, faltering twice along the way, stepping closer to the dull light of his bedroom.

Chapter 18
Childhood

Louise sat on the edge of the bed and waited for her husband to join her. A lone lamp shined on the end table next to her. She had thrown the covers aside, making room for the time when her husband would climb quietly up the stairs to the second floor of their very modest home.

She read from a book absently, like the pages turned without her willing them to do so and the ideas presented were mindless thoughts she did not comprehend.

Her thoughts were distracted by what Gallagher had said to her over coffee that afternoon. She had never given any more thought to Jack Monroe than anyone else in town, that is to say, just as much as anyone else thought of him. Being male and single in small towns like Beaumont was not that unusual and why bother considering it, really. Most people kept their thoughts to themselves about the unusual. It was a politically correct time and Beaumont was no less politically correct than most New England towns, evolved as they liked to think of themselves. Still, Gallagher's words seeped out and distracted Louise as she waited for her husband to join her. What did Hank mean about another trip? He must have been referring to Jack's next trip to Williamsport, but why bother mentioning it? She let her thoughts run on in the darkness

Hank stepped into the bedroom. Louise got up and helped her husband out of his oxford shirt, careful not to disturb his left arm, still fully encased in plaster. As she helped him guide his arm, his fingers caught the edge of his sleeve, sending a pulse of pain down his shoulder and arm. He winced noticeably.

"I'm so sorry, baby. Do you want to do it yourself?"

"No, chief, I think I could use the help."

She took a familiar t-shirt from the top drawer of the dresser and helped him pull it carefully over his head and this time, managed not to hurt her husband's arm. She held the covers for him and he eased into bed. She moved around to the other side and shut off the light. The room was completely dark and it took both of them some time to adjust to the blackness. Neither spoke. After what seemed like hours, Louise decided she needed her husband to open up.

"These weeks have been hard for you, baby."

"Yes."

"The night you drove off, after Ken's funeral, you said it was your fault. I've been thinking about that. Why do you think that way?"

She rolled over onto her side and propped up her head with her left hand. She let the question hover in the darkness. The pack of coyotes they heard a while back was yammering now as they took down their prey, somewhere deep in the fields behind their house. "Please, Hank. What did you mean?"

It took him a few seconds before he spoke.

"I think everyone blames themselves when someone close ends their life the way Ken did."

"It's not something else?"

"I don't know what else to say about it, Louise. He's gone and don't you feel like we're a bit responsible? He was our friend. He was my best friend."

"I don't see how we can blame ourselves, Hank. Ken carried a demon that he kept hidden. No one saw it coming. No one could have done anything. Ken did what he did and as awful as it was, we have to accept it."

"I'm not sure I can do that."

"You're going to have to let it go soon. You're suffering, and I get that, but it wasn't your fault."

"Really?"

"No, it wasn't your fault."

Louise took Hank's hand and held it gently. She needed more information.

"But what about the basketball shoes? Why would Ken leave them behind, Hank?"

"What shoes? You didn't tell me about any basketball shoes."

Hank lay on his back and turned his head to face his wife. He could clearly see her eyes shine in the dark. "What do you mean about the basketball shoes?" Louise realized that she hadn't told him anything about the dead oak and the root ball and the crater where she and Gallagher had found the abandoned Converse All-Stars.

"I'm sorry. You've been so closed off, and I didn't want to bother you, but now I need to know. I found a pair of kids gold, high top Converse All-Star basketball shoes not far from the rope swing, hidden at the bottom of a crater at the big oak not far from the swing. You remember the oak?"

"I do."

"They were the same shoes you've kept, Hank, the ones you have in a box in the attic."

He took a long breath and held it for a few seconds before slowly letting the air escape from his lungs. The beast was forcing its way out again.

"Why would Ken leave his old basketball shoes behind, and in the crater from the root ball?" Louise pressed and looked carefully at her husband in the dark.

Now she was the police chief, carefully observing a suspect. She caught herself thinking that way and tried to shake it off. Her training in the state police had kicked in subconsciously, so it was a challenge to maintain her view of her husband as just that, her husband. The police chief won out.

"Hank?"

He lay motionless in the dark. He had left her and gone off to some other space or time.

"Hank, please."

He turned slightly in the bed and gazed past her, looking out the door onto their terrace. He had traveled far away from her this night, and she desperately wanted to bring him back. She had waited long enough and felt instinctively that something inside Hank needed to be pulled out of a hole. Whatever was tormenting her husband had to be unearthed.

The beast within Hank began to take form again. It raged in his subconscious, fighting to break out. He struggled to hold on to it and keep it tame, but he was tired and the beast grew in his mind. He jumped out of bed, succumbing to the animal and ignoring his broken arm. He raced from the bed and sprinted from the bedroom and out the glass door leading to their porch. Hank's fierce rush startled Louise and she chased after him. She caught him and placed her hands on Hank's shoulders. His entire body shook violently when she touched him. His shaking startled her and she pulled her hands away and backed off. She felt a palpable force pulsing around her husband. It scared her. She tried to break though. Her words came out shallow, like the force surrounding Hank kept her at bay.

"Tell me what's wrong, my god, Hank. Let me in."

"Christ," he shot back at her. He sank to his knees and cried out. The power of his voice seemed to quiet the coyote pack. "I'm breaking inside and I can't keep the beast down."

"What beast? Hank, you're terrifying me."

Louise took another step away. Her eyes bore into the back of his skull. She began to shake with fear. She had never seen her husband this way and the visage of his desperation startled her. She looked upon her husband and saw that he was something very different to her at that moment, something primal and adolescent, a ghost from some phantasmal plane. Hank began to speak, but now his voice was a child's voice, one she remembered from years ago when they first met and raced together in the woods, rode bikes together, and swung from a fat rope, out over a crystal lake, swinging with Mickey Cummings, and Ken Richardson, and other innumerable childhood friends she kept from fading from memory and shadow.

"I am nothing without my friend. Nothing really at all. He is gone and I am here and it makes me sad." Hank continued with his high-pitched, child's voice, like the man inside was gone forever and this boy had taken his place. "I want him back, mommy. I want Ken back."

Louise stepped forward and in spite of her terror over the transfiguration of her husband into a little boy, she kneeled down and put both arms around him and rocked him, like Hank's mom rocked him when he fell off his bike or got hit in the shin with a hockey puck.

"I have you, my darling. I'm holding on. Tell me more."

Louise spoke quietly, lovingly, trying to pull her husband back, but the child's voice remained.

"I didn't like the game tonight, mommy."

"Tell me why."

It just wasn't fun, that's all."

Hank's body began to sag. He gave out a childlike whimper as he fell toward the porch railing. Louise grabbed on tightly and kept him from crashing.

"I don't want to go to Celtics games anymore."

"No, of course not. You don't have to go, ever again sweetie. I've got you, baby. Come back to me, sweet

Hank. Don't go where I cannot follow."

She needed all of her strength to keep him up. He grabbed onto her arms and grunted, but this time, it was Hank's grunt and not that of a broken child.

"Louise, what happened?" He looked around, startled to be where he was and not able to recall what got him there. "Why am I outside on the porch?"

"I don't think you felt very well, baby. You might have a fever, I don't know. You've had a very hard time of late. I think you're just exhausted."

"I think I am. Can I lay down for a bit? I need to find some rest."

"Of course. Let me help you." Louise guided her husband back into the bedroom. He crawled across the bed, climbing over her spot and dropping down onto his, pulling the covers up over his shoulders, even though it was a very hot night in Massachusetts. Louise bent down and kissed her husband. She tucked him in and he began to doze. As she stood back up and watched her husband's chest rise and fall, Hank moved his right hand and placed his thumb in his mouth. He sucked down hard, and for everything Louise had experienced over the last hour or so, the sight of her adult husband, the strongest person she had ever known, first talking in a child's voice and then sucking on his thumb scared her to her marrow. She was witnessing something black and terrible. She wrapped her arms around her husband and prayed that he would come back to her in the morning.

Chapter 19

Mass General

When Louise awoke, she disengaged from her husband and got out of bed to brush her teeth. Her hair was disheveled, and she winced when she looked at herself in the mirror. The skin under her eyes sagged slightly. She wasn't old, but she found it hard to look at a face that had seemed to age over the last month. She scowled and finished brushing her teeth, spitting the bluish residue into her sink. Hank's sink was well kept and tidy, belying the fact that these last two weeks had been so terribly hard on him. She smiled just a bit as she looked at his sink, comparing it to the disaster of her own.

She walked out of the bathroom to where Hank remained in the same position she had left him moments before. Something about seeing him that way, in the exact same position, let loose a warning bell. When she moved to wake him, she noticed that his eyes were slightly open and his thumb remained fixed to the roof of his mouth. Louise let out a gasp as she quickly threw back the covers. The horror of the night before flooded back. Hank was in a fetal position, his chest barely moving up and down. She reached down quickly and shook Hank. A low moan drifted out of him and he pulled his knees up closer to his chest, but he did not seem aware of his surroundings. Louise raced around her side of the bed. She banged her shin. She let out a yelp but fought through it. She grabbed her phone and punched in 9-1-1.

"Please, my husband is not well. Send someone. 75 East Road. This is Chief Louise Consola of the Beaumont police department."

"Chief?" It was Betty, taking her monthly shift at the emergency desk. "Is he breathing? My God, chief."

"Yes, he's breathing, but he's not moving. I don't think he's moved since he fell asleep last night."

"I'm sending an ambulance. Where do you want to take him?"

"Mass General."

"Chief, Lawrence General is so much closer."

"Mass General, for Christ's sake, Betty. Let the ambulance know!"

She hung up her phone and threw it on the bed. She raced back around to Hank and kneeled down next to him. The door opened and the twins stepped in. Pammy dropped her phone on the floor and Gretchen put her hand to her mouth and stifled a scream.

"What's wrong with Daddy?" Gretchen asked as she ran over to her parents' bed. Pammy remained frozen by the doorway.

"Your dad's not feeling well. I called for an ambulance."

"Why is he sucking his thumb?" Pammy yelled as she stepped closer to her father.

"I don't know. We've gotta get him to the hospital. Get

119

your things, both of you. Now."

The girls snapped out of their shock and quickly stepped out the door and down to their bedrooms where they threw on some sweatpants and flip flops.

"I'm here, Hank."

Louise took hold of Hank's left hand. The thumb of his right hand remained firmly in his mouth. Gretchen returned. Her face was pale and she picked at her right arm. Pammy stepped in right behind.

"Go outside, Gretchen, and wait for the ambulance."

"I think it's here, mom."

Gretchen ran down the staircase and opened the front door. A man and a woman walked in, guiding a stretcher on wheels.

"He's up there."

Gretchen stepped out of the way as the two EMTs climbed up the staircase. Pammy stood outside her parents' bedroom and pointed. The EMT's slid the stretcher into the bedroom. Betty appeared at the door. Her voice was hushed as she spoke to the EMTs.

"Be careful," Betty said.

The female EMT kneeled down and took Hank's pulse while the other EMT spoke to him.

"Mr. Consola, can you hear me?"

He looked at Hank's face. Hank's breathing remained shallow and he did not stir at the mention of his name.

"Let's move him to the ambulance. The dispatcher said

Mass General, is that right?"

Louise nodded quickly and moved aside, letting the EMT's wheel Hank into the hallway, down the stairs, and out to the ambulance.

"I'll take the girls, chief. We'll meet you there." Betty took the hands of Gretchen and Pammy. Both of the twins shook now, full of fear at what had become of their father.

"Thank you, Betty. Girls, come here." Louise held her girls close. "Your dad will be fine. He's been through a great deal. We all have."

She let go of the girls. Before she left the house, she bent down and opened the safe. She pulled out her service revolver and holster and placed them in a backpack. She slung it over her shoulder quickly and hopped into the ambulance, kneeling next to her husband as the door slammed shut. The ambulance drove off as neighbors stood outside in pajamas and flip flops and wondered what other terrible things might the Consola family have to endure.

"Coach asked me to go fishing with him," Ken said, early in the morning after a nighttime's gentle rain. Hank sat at the picnic table behind his house while Ken threw a rubber ball against the side of Hank's garage. He looked at his friend, catching the ball expertly with bare hands, pivoting to make another throw. Hank returned the gaze. He breathed in deeply, subconsciously, fearfully. Ken continued to throw the ball against the garage, his gold Converse-All Stars muddied with each toss.

Chapter 20

Cape Cod

Jack Monroe had important things to consider. Very important things. His perfect world was beginning to unravel, like a spool of twine toyed with by an old cat. The strands were tightly bound to the spool, but now the old cat had played at it enough that the twine was laid bare, frayed and disintegrating. The chief had brought the basketball shoes to Jack's house. Such fine, damning shoes. She knew, or she might soon know. That couldn't happen. He was a hero and he deserved all that he had earned, all that he had taken. And Gallagher, so quiet and so invasive, looking at Jack like a great-horned owl spies a skunk. And he had another trip coming up. A delicious trip. He had been working on it for months, since the last trip, since the last little boy. The thought of Tommy Timmons aroused him and his mind traveled to the hotel room they would share.

He sat at his kitchen table. He felt the familiar swell within his khakis as the thought of last year's trip took hold; this year's trip and all that he would take.

He thought some more and considered Mickey Cummings. No one knew about Mickey being gay, and Jack knew Mickey wanted to keep it that way. Still, Mickey was one of his boys, one who could squeal, not like that one time at the motel but in a way where others could hear him squeal. Yes, he needed to consider Mickey Cummings. He was part of the frayed twine that might need to be rewound, tighter this time and then tied off so it couldn't be unwound again.

Jack looked back to his roster. The throbbing in his crotch did not dissipate.

Mickey Cummings sat in the darkness of his office. It was close to midnight. A bottle of dependable scotch sat mostly empty on his desk. He held his head in his cigar-stained hands. Ken's death was a haunting for him. So was Hank's accident. And Mickey's own secrets. Both of them; the one from long ago and the one he carried like a stone on his bent back. His head grew heavier, pushing down on his hands until he felt like it could not be held up any longer. He laughed, grimly. Did he really think he could maintain the layer of secrecy which would keep him safe, keep him mayor?

Louise had called. Hank was in the hospital and he wasn't doing well. He wasn't responding to anyone. He was in the psych ward and the doctors had given him sedatives. Louise thought they might relax Hank so he might sleep and then wake up and talk. Louise sounded frightened, the first time she had ever sounded that way to Mickey. She was buckling under the strain. To be expected, of course. Even the strongest flowers wilted in heavy rain.

Mickey tilted the bottle back and drained the last of the clear liquid. He put the bottle down, careful to place it far enough away from the edge of his mahogany desk so as not to knock it over with a careless hand. He reached down to the bottom drawer and opened it up, pushing around papers and some files. He found nothing. He searched the rest of his drawers until he realized that there was no more booze. He was alone with no more comfort from the bottle. Slowly, almost imperceptibly, a fear in him began to ascend, rising up from his gut. His heart began to race in spite of the alcohol.

First Ken and then Hank almost getting killed, and now he lay prostrate in a psych ward in Boston. The thoughts began to form, in a fog at first and then more clearly, like the shape of a stranger forms in the dark, pressing down on you as you walk by. The basketball shoes, Ken, Hank, himself, and Jack Monroe. Home-town hero Jack Monroe. He was the common denominator to everything from the last few weeks. Jack and his boys. Was Ken Richardson one of Jack Monroe's boys, just like Mickey? The basketball shoes, perfect and gold and brutal in their outward innocence. Ken kept them, an heirloom to his horror. The image was clear to him now, proof that Mickey's nightmare was not a solitary one. Jack Monroe had to have raped Ken. It was obvious now.

It might have been some consolation, but a rape is not a shared horror. It is as particular in its evil as the difference between dead flowers in a field, early morning flowers robbed of their life, ruined before their time to blossom.

It had only happened that one time, in that one motel room, on that one singularly destructive trip to the Cape.

And years later, when he had become mayor, he had been indiscrete, and somehow, there was Jack Monroe coming into Mickey's office. He had a video and wouldn't that be pretty if the town found out that Mickey Cummings was the newly elected gay mayor of Beaumont when none of

Beaumont was really ready to accept such a notion, at least back then. Perhaps if Mickey had come out before he ran for office, the town would have shown their liberal propensities and shrugged it off. But that was long ago and Mickey had lived with the horror of Jack Monroe. Now what was he supposed to do? He just gave him the keys to the city. Too many townsfolk had put forth Jack's name, and Mickey saw the political downside to keeping Jack off the list, so he had to lay prostrate to the town and let Jack be so honored. He had swallowed much to become mayor, and what he knew to be the truth about Jack Monroe was a most bitter pill. How does one get out from behind that rock? Yes, you're our hometown hero and I've known all along that you were a monster. There is no real surviving that.

No, Mickey sucked on his cigar that day and kept the town safe from itself. There was nothing he could do. His impotence was complete and he had long known that he had raped his own town almost as completely as he had been raped as a little boy. He slammed his fist down and the power of the sound was heard by absolutely no one at all in the quiet of the town offices. Blood seeped out of his knuckles and he let it flow without trying to staunch his wound. He tried to cry out but no sound emanated from the visage of a scream from his twisted face. He looked like that man on the bridge, that painting, screaming in horror with no one near to help ease the pain.

Louise had sent the girls home from the hospital with Betty a few hours ago. They complained, but there was nothing they could do for their dad, so her mother convinced them to go home. The doctor had told Louise that Hank was in the middle of a psychiatric trauma, perhaps some PTSD long held dormant. He hoped that the meds he gave Hank would help him relax and even sleep and perhaps that would end the event and he could talk to Louise and share the depth of his pain, but the doctor didn't know how long that would take, perhaps hours or days.

"Has he had any trauma recently?" The doctor sat with Louise in the family waiting area. It was early morning so they had the room to themselves.

"Yes, doctor. His best friend committed suicide a few weeks ago and then Hank was in a crash the night of his friend's funeral." She held back the fact that the state police had discovered that her husband's break lines had been cut.

"Of course. That's a great deal for anyone to bear. All of his vitals are strong, so we're hoping there are no physical issues to deal with. In cases like this, sometimes there are, but I think we don't need to worry about that right now. My main concern is the condition of your husband when you brought him in. It was as extreme a case of psychological breakdown as I've seen in a while. Most people who exhibit symptoms like that show some kind of manifestations, at least mild ones, well before an acute event occurs. I'm hopeful his acute symptoms will end just as quickly, but to be honest, he is just going to need time." He looked at her for a bit. Louise sat ramrod straight in her chair. Seeing her husband curled up in a fetal position and sucking his thumb had almost broken her and the girls. Selfishly, she needed to hold herself upright and firm to keep herself from falling apart, chief of police or not.

"Thank you, doctor. Can I stay with him?"

"Certainly. Let me get someone to set up a cot in Hank's room. Rest if you can. As I said, Hank might come out of his event today or maybe in a week. He is a strong man, Louise. We just have to be patient." The doctor stood up and shook Louise' hand and walked out of the family room. He put his phone to his ear and took another call.

Louise felt a wave of exhaustion course through her and felt herself begin to slide down her chair. She bit her lip and tried not to cry. It was hard being alone, but she was glad that the waiting area was empty. If she wanted to cry, this was the time. The remaining strength she had began to ebb and her self control was nearly depleted. Tears welled in her eyes. She was about to let go when she heard footsteps move through the hallway. Gallagher came in and sat down beside her. She took her hands and quickly wiped the tears from her eyes.

"I just heard. How's he doing?" Gallagher sat down next to her.

"Not very well. The doctor doesn't know when Hank might come around." Gallagher folded his arms. The two sat silently, the hum of the hospital barely registering.

"Chief, I know there is no good time to bring this up, but I can't get Jack Monroe out of my head."

"I've been thinking about him as well." Louise glanced out of the large window overlooking the parking lot seven floors below. City traffic moved up and down. They didn't slow down for yellow lights and occasional horns blared in protest.

"Everything seems tied to Monroe; your husband, Ken

Richardson, the mayor, the kids basketball shoes."

"I know. I'm trying to focus on my husband, but you think this is all connected."

"I think we'd be remiss if we didn't consider the connections."
"Jesus, Gallagher, I'm exhausted right now. Would you mind if we talk about this tomorrow? Maybe I'll know more about Hank by then."

"Of course. Let me know if there is anything I can do." Gallagher got up and left the room, placing his strong hand on her shoulder as he passed into the hallway.

Louise sat back up and tucked her feet under her body. She wiped her eyes of the tears that had formed after Gallagher left. A few people had entered the family room at the hospital. She sure as hell didn't want to have them see her cry, even though she was sure they were going through their own hell.

Before Betty took the girls home, Louise sat down with them to talk about their daddy and what he was going through.

"It's going to be your decision how or if you want to share what's going on with your dad with your friends. You are young women and I'm not going to tell you what to do about this. Your friends might be a real comfort for you, and then again, they may not."

"Why might they not be, mom? They have been my best friends forever. I tell them everything."

Pammy got up and paced. Gretchen nodded her head but kept her eyes down, staring at her pink toenails protruding from her flip flops.

"You have to understand that some people look at mental illness like they might catch it. They don't understand that the mind is simply another one of God's gifts, and when the mind is sick, many of the visible signs of its illness are seen in the odd behavior of the person. Some people can't or won't see it for what it is; an illness. They use words like "mental" or "crazy" and that is so unfortunate. Your dad's illness right now is no different than if he was having appendicitis. No one makes fun of people with appendicitis, but our world isn't set up for people to be accepting of mental illness. There are too many things in this world that people want to hide away. Too many things," she sighed.

Louise stood up and pulled the twins close.

"Your dad isn't crazy. He's a healthy man with a mind that is coping with a serious trauma. The doctors will take care of your dad, and when he comes around, you do the same. Don't treat him like he's broken. Treat him with the love he deserves, the way you have always treated your father." The twins held their mother closer. Betty waited off to the side, nodding her head in agreement. She thought the chief's words were meant for her as much as for the twins. "Now go home. Make good decisions about how or if you want to share the news about your dad. Just don't think everyone will be evolved enough to handle the news properly. Are you ready to deal with that?"

"We are," the girls and even Betty chimed in.

"Good, I'll see you in the morning. I love you, you know that, and so does your father, and he'll be fine. Believe me."

"We do," the twins, and Betty, responded together. Now

all four of them hugged and finally, Betty led the twins out of the family area.

That was hours ago. Louise was content with how she handled it with the girls. She wasn't so sure other people would be so compassionate when the news leaked out about Hank. Social media being the way it was, she sure as hell knew that it would leak out. She sighed and stood up. She reached her hands high above her head and arched her back, stretching the taut muscles that ran along the length of her neck. She stepped out of the family room and walked down the hall, past nurses focused on their patients and an occasional doctor checking computerized charts. She stood outside Hank's room, took a deep breath, and pushed open the doors. She took up a chair and sat next to him. He continued to sleep. His thumb from his right hand had slid out of his mouth and rested against his chin, spittle dripping down onto his wrist. Maybe a good sign. Chief Louise Consola folded her arms and fell off into sleep. It had been almost a day since she had found Hank comatose, fetal and sucking on his thumb. Later that night, when the hospital was quiet and the hallways had been darkened, when she finally woke, she was surprised that she was able to fall asleep at all.

Chapter 21

Williamsport

The families gathered at Jack's house. Fifteen families with fifteen, bright-eyed, joyous, naive boys. Jack passed out the itinerary for the trip to Williamsport. There were picnics planned, a trip to an amusement park, swimming, exchanging Little League pins with other towns, sliding on the hill behind center field, hikes, movies, and all the baseball a young boy could consume. This was the American dream, and perhaps, one day, Jack's boys might be good enough to make it to the World Series themselves, to play in the tournament, be the center of the universe, be bright shining stars. That's what he told all of them as they enjoyed their afternoon at Jack Monroe's home.

The parents ate it up. How generous and loving for this man to want to give of himself so selflessly, so completely to the boys he had dedicated all of his free time.

Ice cream and cake were eaten by all. The boys jumped and frolicked in Jack's new pool, its installation long planned to coincide with the picnic. There was a diving board, curved slide, and hot tub situated off the edge of the shallow end of the pool. Bright blue and gold bobbers marked the demarcation between the safe, shallow end and the severe vertical plunge into the deepest part of the pool. Jack sat on a cheap lawn chair, drinking beer and enjoying the scene as fifteen boys splashed each other and played pool basketball, throwing a nerf ball at a floating hoop. He delighted in the joy the boys felt, as did their parents. Americana perfected.

His delight was very different from what the parents felt. His long, thought-out plan was now close to fruition. He had only to keep up the facade, just a few days more. His toad brain squirmed at the perfection of his machinations.

Two of the younger boys swam around using inflatable rings to keep them afloat. Such sweet boys, so eager for playing time. Jack spied their sinuous legs and slim, immature fingers. A throb pulsed through his midsection which he deftly covered with a can of beer. He adjusted his black glasses, making sure the elastic that kept them on his face was properly fastened. He moved his hand with the beer, adjusting it so the cold aluminum can rested on his thigh. His pleasure was now obscured and he laughed as the two boys, the youngest of boys, splashed water on each other. Their parents, oh those innocent, naive, synthetic parents. They believed in the perfect future of their children and the certainty of their athletic gifts. They were blind to the realities of their children's future, so willing to give them every, single, possible, erroneous opportunity and advantage, to give their kids the proverbial leg up over the competition. Jack Monroe was their child's leg up. Being on his team almost guaranteed access to elite tournaments, college exposure, and high school playing time. Blindspotting.

The trip was just days away and Jack Monroe could not possibly be more satisfied with how everything was going according to plan.

Chapter 22

Breakdown

The late afternoon cast long, reaching shadows into Hank's hospital room. Louise sat at the end of her husband's bed. There had been little change. Hank would rally once in a while, stirring in his bed, tucked in purposefully with drab, overused pillows. The room was decorated with get well cards from the girls and the precinct and Hank's friends from work. When he shifted in his bed, Louise was quick to move to his side, holding his hand and dabbing his furrowed brow with a damp cloth. Once Hank murmured as he moved around in bed. "My, my fault...all of it," and he would thrash about, violently, until the fit passed. The nurse would come in and check the IV that dripped steadily into Hank's forearm. It was a mild sedative, helping Hank sleep, hopefully easing his mind back to a better place. Whatever dreams raged in his mind manifested with low moans and contortions of his body. Louise held his hands and kissed his face gently when the fit would subside. There was no way for her to break the pain her husband endured in his private, ethereal hell.

Louise left the running of the police department to Betty. She checked in with Louise now and again to make sure Hank hadn't become worse, but the doctors all said patience and hope was needed right now and Hank would return to them when his mind would allow it, probably in a few days. Louise had gone home once when Gallagher came in to sit with Hank. She stunk and the women's side of her cried for a shower. When she couldn't stand herself any longer, she broke down and went home. She slept fitfully in her own bed, waking up to throw her arm over Hank's bare leg. She bolted when she realized that Hank had not recovered and still lay, tormented, in his hospital bed back in Boston. She stared up at the ceiling, not capable of sleeping. She lay awake, searching the recesses of her mind to try to piece together the maze of the last few weeks. Jack Monroe. Her mind continued to struggle with the puzzle piece of Jack Monroe. Gallagher had his suspicions and now his ideas pushed forward from the recesses of her psyche. Coach, friend to all, home-town hero, idol to the boys. And there were fifteen more of them ready to romp off to Williamsport with him in just a few days.

A thin film of sweat began to form on Louise' forehead. Her breathing became strained as she flashbacked to finding Ken, bloated, sprawled and bleeding, eyes pecked out and gashes in his legs laid bare to the baking sun, naked to the pecks of birds, on the same day as the town honored Jack for his devotion to the boys in town. A dark thought began to push its way out, a thought that needed attention.

Louise sat up quickly in the blackness of her and Hank's bedroom. She jumped off the bed and hurried into the bathroom. She quickly undressed and stepped under the stream of water coursing from the powerful jets of the shower. She scrubbed away the stink from too many nights at the hospital. She worked shampoo quickly through her hair, rinsing it out thoroughly. She stepped out of the shower, toweled off, and stood in front of the mirror. She applied a hint of eyeliner and ran the hair dryer until she could brush her hair back to reasonableness. She brushed her teeth, hard, eliciting a little blood from the flossing she had neglected to do of late. She stepped out of her bathroom and put on her police uniform. When all was set, she turned to leave her room when Pammy and Gretchen stepped in. They were roused by the hair dryer and startled when their alarm pulsed 3:30 AM like a bat signal, bright on their ceiling. Their mother never got up this early.

"Mom, what are you doing? It's, like, 3:30," Gretchen yawned as she leaned on the frame surrounding the door into her parents' room.

"Where are you going?" Pammy flopped on her parent's bed, eyes fading under heavy lids.

"I need to talk to the mayor. You'll be fine here. I won't be long, and then I'll come back and pick you up and we'll all go to see your dad."

"Why do you need to see Mayor Cummings?" Pammy sat back up on the bed, rallying at the ludicrousness of the time and the notion of waking up Mickey Cummings so early in the morning.

"I want to talk to him about your father and uncle Ken. They all played together. Maybe he can tell me something more, but more likely he'll just add to my confusion."

"Can't it wait until a reasonable hour, like ten in the morning?"

"Me getting up this early embarrassing you, Pammy?"

"A little," she laughed and reached down to her

omnipresent cell phone.

Her thumbs moved incredibly fast as she responded to the latest Instagram post or Twitter feed. Better not to miss a thing.

"Well, this isn't the first time I've embarrassed the both of you, my loves. Still, I need to see the mayor. Go back to bed and I'll wake you when I return. Leave the phones here."

"Mother!" they both complained as they handed over their lifelines to the chief.

Their bodies shook almost imperceptibly as their crack was taken away from them. They groaned as they left their parent's bedroom and flopped back into their own beds.

Chapter 23

Pillow Talk

Louise drove out toward Mickey Cumming's home, down route 28, almost to the North Reading border. It was still dark, with no other car on the road except a lone dump truck traveling north. The two vehicles passed, the dump truck high beams momentarily blinding Louise. She hit her horn and held it down. She looked in her rear-view mirror. The truck ignored her, high beams illuminating the darkness. "Prick," she muttered. She was no happier driving this early in the morning than the truck driver.

She finally arrived in Mickey's neighborhood. She pulled her cruiser in the driveway, careful to turn her lights off. She got out of her cruiser and knocked on Mickey's door. She waited a bit before knocking again, this time putting a bit more force into it. She shifted her feet and instinctively checked her firearm, secured properly at her hip. She had no reason to do this other than the habit she had developed when entering anyone's house. Some things cops don't stop doing. Finally, dressed in a silk bathrobe, Mickey opened the door.

"What the hell, chief? It's four in the morning."

"Can I speak with you, Mickey?"

He stepped aside to let Louise into his mudroom and then the open-concept kitchen. Louise looked around. His home was spotless, with steel appliances properly polished and rows of pots and pans hanging from copper hooks embedded in a beam that ran the length of the kitchen ceiling. There was a center isle with a sink and cutting board. Mickey had a collection of wines placed carefully in a glass and gold wine console. Two glasses, mostly empty, sat on a rich oak kitchen table adjacent to an alcove leading out to a solarium.

"Yes, I have a guest." Mickey picked up the two wine glasses and placed them in his sink. He sat down at his kitchen table and motioned for Louise to join him. "Can we make this short?"

"Sure, Mr. Mayor. Anyone I know?" she asked mischievously.

"Most assuredly not." Mickey crossed one leg over the other and rested the back of his head against the wall. His eyes were bloodshot, and Louise surmised that it wasn't only a few glasses of wine Mickey and his guest had consumed the night before. "How is Hank?"

"Not well, to be honest, and that's why I wanted to talk to you."

"At four in the morning? Christ."

"Yes, at four in the morning."

"So it couldn't wait until office hours?" Louise looked hard at the mayor. "Of course, it couldn't. That was a dumb question."

"Tell me more about Jack Monroe."

Mickey uncrossed one leg and replaced it with another. His

foot began to bob. He shifted his weight so he could untuck his silk robe that had been stuck under his thigh. Louise watched Mickey move about and waited a few more moments. "Mickey?"

"You know everything about him, our hometown hero. What would you have me add?"

"I don't know. Gallagher seems to think something is amiss with Jack. We stopped by his house a few days ago and showed him the same basketball shoes I showed you in my office. He seemed startled when we showed him the shoes. He wouldn't even touch them. Any reason that might be?"

"Shit, they were the shoes we all wore, and Ken had just died. I'm sure the sight of the shoes shook him up. They shook me up."

"Still, I understood his response for what it was, a coach devastated by the loss of one of his own, but Gallagher seemed to think Jack's reaction was strange, almost like it was defensive, like something about the shoes bothered him. Do you have any thoughts on that?" Mickey folded his hands like you do when praying and crossed his leg again. He looked through his kitchen out into the solarium. The early-dawn light had begun to illuminate ferns and bamboo plants. They were moist from Mickey's spritzing them the night before. A single leaf hung precariously from its twig and then its tenuous bind became too weak to hold it up. It fluttered silently and landed on a footstool next to one of Mickey's chairs in the solarium. He shook his head, slightly, like he was driving a thought out of his consciousness. He cleared his throat and coughed, holding his tobacco-stained hand over his mouth. Louise watched carefully and waited. It was quiet in Mickey's kitchen except for a grandfather clock that ticked away in the next room. The noise of the clock seemed to echo throughout the house. Louise thought she could hear Mickey's heart pound through his bathrobe.

"He knows."

"He knows what, Mickey?"

"He knows I'm gay." For the third time, Mickey crossed his legs again.

"I know you're gay."

"Yes. But you've kept my secret because you are a kind, wonderful soul, chief Louise Consola."

"And Jack Monroe is not?"

"Our hometown hero?" Jack stood up and walked into his solarium.

Louise followed and they sat down, facing each other as the sun began its steady rise through the trees behind Mickey's home.

"Tell me."

"So many things to hide, so many things," he spoke almost to himself.

"That's rather cryptic, Mickey."

"I'm sorry. It's early, chief. You showing up like this, so very early in the morning, hasn't allowed my brain to work properly." Mickey sat up and put his elbows on his knees. His head remained bowed and he ran his fingers through his white hair. "He has a video."

"Excuse me?"

"When I first became mayor, I was less than discrete. I met a man in a motel in Boston, can't remember his face any more, to be honest. I don't know how, but Jack was there and he took a video of me kissing the man. I can't even remember who he was or what he looked like, but Jack showed up in my office a few days later and told me about the video. He said it would help me keep the other secret safe." Louise stood up and bending over, picked up the lone leaf that had fluttered to the floor not minutes before. She looked at it carefully and then sat back down. She crossed her own legs. Her gun sat snuggly at her side and she shifted her weight so as not to put any pressure on the holster. She slipped the leaf into her pants pocket.

"I don't understand."

"Maybe there's a great deal you don't understand."

"What possible reason would Jack Monroe have for taking a video of you with another man in some sleazy motel in Boston?"

"You make it sound so dirty, chief."

"Sorry. That came out wrong."

"This is all a bit too much for me so early on a work day."

"I'm sorry it's so hard, but Mickey, no one would care if your secret came out."

"Are you sure? We all have secrets that we have to keep, Louise. All of us do."

"You're being cryptic again, Mickey."

"Jesus, Louise, isn't it enough that I could be destroyed if the people of our fair town found out I had hidden my sexuality from them, after so many elections when I stood before them and claimed to be something I was not?"

"You've been a fine mayor, Mickey. Everyone knows that. What could you have possibly done that would shame you? I've seen all the good you've done for this town. I've seen the quiet ways you've helped out when no one was looking. I've seen you at your best. I think you pump too many hands for votes sometimes, but that comes with the territory. You've been a wonderful mayor. You've always held Beaumont's interests in your highest regard."

"Well, maybe not always. Sometimes we have to destroy ourselves in order to save ourselves."

"You've lost me again, Mickey. Stop speaking in riddles, for God's sake."

"Louise, you know that old saying, 'We're all stronger in the broken places?'

"Yes, I've heard that before"

"I think that it is a lie."

"Where are you broken, Mickey? It certainly isn't because you're gay."

Mickey stood up suddenly. He wrapped his silk robe tightly around his body, like something inside was struggling to get out and the thinness of the fabric was straining at the seams. He looked out of his solarium into the darkness of the trees, contrasting with the halo that had begun to form around the forest as the sun began to rise.

"When did you get introduced to sex, Louise?"

"I'm sorry?"

"When did you get introduced to sex?"

Mickey sat back down and leaned back in his chair. It was royal blue and the corduroy fabric matched wonderfully with the green plants growing peacefully about the solarium.

"What do my sexual experiences have to do with Jack Monroe?"

"Humor me, Louise, please. You'll see where I am going with this rather contorted line of questioning."

"And my response has something to do with Jack Monroe and the basketball shoes?"

"It does, if you would let me get you there."

"Alright."

She turned in her chair and touched one of the bamboo plants growing from a large pot. It was smooth except for where growth rings spiraled on the outside of the fibrous trunk. She took her hand away and turned back to Mickey.

"It was Ken Richardson. We went to a movie, not too long before I started dating Hank. The sex was awkward and clumsy and was mostly my doing. It happened quickly and we were both startled when it was over. Ken kept apologizing, like it was dirty or something. It wasn't good, but it wasn't dirty. We sat awkwardly in his car until we both started to laugh, like we couldn't believe this was our first time and it happened with each other. He drove me home and we sat in my driveway for hours, talking about our dreams and the things we felt important in our lives. I kissed him on the cheek, and he smiled kindly, but there was a hint of sadness in his smile, like even though we had just had sex for the first time, it bothered him, and he might have wished he could pull it back. But then his face brightened when I told him not to be so dramatic. The world was a fine place and we were lucky to be part of it. He laughed some more and then I got out and he drove off. And that was it. When we saw each other around school, it was like it never happened, or it was like it did happen and we recognized it for what it was; simple sexual explorations that perhaps went a bit too far and too quickly.

"I even told Hank after we were married. He didn't get mad at all, now that I think about it. As a matter of fact, I think Hank was pleased with the idea that Ken had made out with a girl. So that's how it happened for me."

"Louise, I always knew I was gay. But it wasn't something shared in Beaumont back then, and it certainly wasn't something shared with the guys on the team."

"Ken and Hank."

"That's right. I wasn't part of their inner circle, let's just say. How do you function when the two best players on the team are people you're attracted to? It was a secret I needed to keep. No one ever suspected, never mind found out. Maybe it was because of Hank and Ken that I never shared my sexuality with anyone. Shit, I don't know how you figured it out, Louise."

"Well, I am a trained officer of the law, Mickey. I would never share that information with anyone. Especially after how emphatic you were about it when we talked at the hospital the day Hank got in his accident. But why admit it to me then, Mickey?"

"Do you want some coffee?" Mickey began to stand up. Louise motioned for him to sit back down.

"I want to understand the labyrinth of the maze you've started me down."

"So your introduction to sex was rather typical, wouldn't you agree?"

"Sure. Clumsy, but typical."

The sun now burst through the trees and illuminated the solarium in pleasant rays. The room began to warm. Mickey reached over to a spritzer and began his daily nourishing of his plants. Louise sat in her chair and waited for Mickey to complete his morning ritual and resume his riddle.

"Were you hurt by it, the sex with Ken? Did it fuck you up, in a manner of speaking?"

"No, I was sixteen. Most of my friends had made out already. I liked Ken and the boy could play basketball and baseball. He was handsome and one of my best friends and it just happened. We let it go, quickly, like I think it was supposed to be let go. We stayed friends even when I started dating Hank. It was the way most first times happen, I guess."

"I guess," Mickey laughed grimly and let his legs slide out a bit from his chair. "But not everyone starts out in such an innocent way, Louise. You understand that, right? Were all your girlfriends ok with their first time?"

"Of course not. Some felt like it was expected of them."

"You mean it wasn't their choice."

"Yes."

"You mean they were raped."

Another leaf dislodged from the same plant. It landed harshly this time, devoid of sound yet enormous in its crash. Both Louise and Mickey shifted their gaze away from each other and reacted to the leaf.

"What are you trying to say, Mickey?" She looked back up to him. A ray of understanding began to form in the back of her mind and then crystallized. "My God, you were raped, Mickey?"

"Yes."

"Who raped you?"

"It can never come out, Louise. You have to promise me you'll hold what I'm about to tell you to your grave. Swear to me, chief."

"But if you were raped…"

"Swear, chief."

"Ok, of course, I swear."

Mickey sat back down in his chair and looked out as a single beam of sun cut through the forest.

"Jack Monroe raped me."

Louise took a quick, short breath and held it. She looked at Mickey's sad eyes and waited.

"We were on the Cape, playing basketball against a bunch

of travel teams. I wasn't getting much playing time. When it came time on the first night to pick roommates, no one picked me. There were thirteen guys on the team. Why the hell would Jack pick thirteen players for a travel team? It took me a while to think that through, but then I realized that I was the lucky one," he laughed again. "I was the one being targeted."

"You roomed with Jack."

"I roomed with Jack. He said we should watch a movie. It came on and it was this porn movie. A bunch of sweaty men. I was frozen in place with embarrassment as they bumped and ground into each other. Jack was next to me, cheese doodles on the bed and him with his hand in his pants. I couldn't fucking believe it. Finally, the movie ended. I rolled over and tried to pretend to go to sleep. I must have slept a little. I remember waking up and having this terrible weight on top of me. I was on my stomach and he just kept pushing. I couldn't even scream. I didn't know what was happening and my face was buried into my pillow. He put his hands on my shoulders and pushed me down even harder. He let out this terrible sound and then it was over. He rolled off of me and I heard him snore just a few minutes later. Classy man. I never fell back to sleep, I was so shocked and confused.

The next morning, he didn't say a word about it. He bought the team breakfast and he didn't even look at me. He made stupid jokes and the rest of the team laughed. I think I even laughed. I was ten or eleven. I didn't know that I shouldn't laugh. I was in a fog and I didn't know how to act, so I just laughed along with the rest of the team as Monroe made one stupid joke after another. I wish I could have understood what had happened to me, I would have killed him. But I didn't understand so I just sat there and laughed along."

Mickey looked back from the forest. He pulled his robe tighter. His face was expressionless in the light of his solarium.

"So that was how I was introduced to sex."

"My god, Mickey, that wasn't sex."

"So perhaps you see why I can't let on that I'm gay? Can you imagine being introduced to sex in that way, then growing up and having sex with other men, and then the man who raped you shows up with a fucking video tape. He was a god, for Christ's sake. And then the hometown hero thing happened, and Ken dies the same day, and me giving Jack the fucking keys to the city. Hell, I even stood behind him and clapped after I put the medal around his neck. No, chief, this shit can never come out. You have to promise me."

Mickey's eyes closed and he began to cry, barely at first and then the dam burst and he began to sob uncontrollably, his shoulders shaking. He held his hands to his face. He let out five or six brutal, anguished cries, like he was raging at the forest and the trees might break at their base. Louise stood up from her chair and moved quickly to Mickey, kneeling down next to him and holding his hands as he labored to regain his composure.

"And you've told no one else about the rape?"

"That's right. Not even my mother. She knows I'm gay, but she doesn't know about the rape."

"Jack Monroe raped you when you were a little boy and you've kept this to yourself?"

Mickey's crying began to lessen, and his shoulders stopped convulsing.

"The shame was too much. I never told my family, not my friends, the few real ones I actually had. I don't know why I'm telling you. Too much wine last night, perhaps. Too early in the morning for me to check my tongue. Louise, you have to understand, I didn't know I would become mayor."

"Mickey, it was a crime. What am I supposed to do about it now, keep it to myself? I'm the dam chief of police. Don't you think if he raped you he might have raped other little boys? Jesus."

Mickey stood up quickly and pushed her away, a bit too hard. Louise struggled to maintain her balance. The tallest of the bamboo plants crashed, sending shards flying from the shattered pottery. The rich, dark soil that kept the bamboo growing exploded across Mickey's oriental rug. One dark cloud moved across the sky, blotting out the early morning rays of sun.

"Christ, Mick!"

She squatted down and started picking up the broken pottery, cutting her finger on the tiniest of shards. A single drop of blood formed and Louise quickly put her finger in her mouth to stop the bleeding. Mickey left the room and came back with a dust buster. On his hands and knees, he vacuumed the spilled potting soil. He lay fully prone on his stomach as he reached under his chair to collect the last

Rick Collins

remnant of the explosion. Instead of standing up, he remained face down. He began crying again, soundless and muffled and more terribly than before the bamboo plant went flying. His form might have looked similar to the way he looked, pinned down under Jack Monroe, powerless under his assault. Finally, he got up on his hands and knees and looked back into Louise' eyes.

"What you are supposed to do, chief, is honor my request. The town would be shattered to know that they had a monster in their midst and that the mayor has known about it for decades."

"I can't keep this to myself, Mickey. You know I can't."

"I'll kill myself if it comes out, Louise. You know that I will kill myself if I even think this thing even has the slightest possibility of coming out."

"Don't say that."

"I won't survive it. Hell, Ken couldn't survive it."

"What are you saying, Mickey?"

"I don't know, Louise, I'm not sure of anything, but you have to wonder about the timing of Ken's death. Was it a coincidence, Ken killing himself the day we honored our dear hometown hero? And your husband, for God's sake. He is a strong man, but now he's sucking his thumb in the hospital, not more than two weeks after he buried his best friend. And we both know the brakes on his car were cut. Put it all together, chief. Just put it all together."

Louise looked out of the solarium. The dark cloud moved off and another powerful beam of light from the sun almost blinded her. She covered her eyes and looked back toward

150

Mickey.

"What if, Mickey? If it's all true, you're saying Jack Monroe raped you, Ken Richardson killed himself and you think he was raped by Jack too, and then he tried to kill my husband?"

"There's a very dark edge to our town, chief. And you cannot say a word about it."

"But if you're right, might Jack do something horrible again? Are we just supposed to let it happen, to save your reputation?"

"Keeping my secrets is saving the town, chief. The blackness of me is protecting the town from itself."

Mickey stood up. He looked like a deflated balloon, his shoulders sagging and his hands hanging by his side, and clearly, he had had enough. He walked through his kitchen and opened the front door. Their conversation was over.

"Don't you believe that I'm worth protecting?" he asked as he opened the door for the chief. Louise stepped to the door. She turned quickly and gently kissed Mickey on the cheek.

"I don't know what to do, Mickey."

"I'll be destroyed."

"Mickey, my God, there's another trip to Williamsport in a few days."

"Maybe he's gotten it out of his system? Maybe this was just something from his past that he's extinguished."

"Do you believe that, Mickey? Do you believe that about

monsters? Because that's what I don't believe. Monsters don't grow halos."

"You have to protect me, chief. You have to protect the town, and maybe even the memory of Ken. You might even be protecting your husband."

She looked at him, standing in his silk bathrobe. The sun broke enthusiastically through the tops of the trees. In a quickness that surprised her, she slapped Mickey Cummings across the face. She watched him hold up his hands, bracing for another blow. She fought with the impulse to punch him, again, and again, until his face was a bloody pulp and the eyes in his head were gouged out and thrown away like garbage in the woods. She looked at him and hated what she saw and hated everything about her town.

Fighting off her spectral vision, she spun and walked down his driveway and opened the door to her cruiser. She turned the key and the engine came to life. She backed out of the driveway and turned the cruiser into the sun and drove off toward her home. As Mickey's house disappeared behind her, she looked out her windshield. A kindness of vultures circled not far away, high above the grasping trees. Something dank and worthless had died in the forest the night before. The cruel birds began their slow, deliberate spiraling down to pick at the dead creature's flesh.

Chapter 24

Secrets

Gallagher met Louise at a bar named Jake's not far from the hill that ran on up to the academy and the different world of the people of wealth and privilege who stalked about the school and sometimes the town with impervious perfection. The two sat in a booth, hard with dried booze now permanently shellacked into the table. Crude words were carved with expensive butter knives, familiar words like "fuck you" and "eat shit" and other lovely colloquialisms that seemed so inappropriate for such a fine, evolved town such as Beaumont.

Gallagher sat and sipped a beer. Louise picked at a Rueben sandwich and took small sips of coffee from a porcelain mug. She was on duty, although it wouldn't have been the first time the chief of police imbibed on the job.

"There's a very dark thing in this town, Gallagher."

"There's something dark in every town, chief. Why would Beaumont be any different?"

"I always believed our little town sat on a shining hill, calling out to hopeful souls to join the ranks of our chosen."

"That's rather prosaic for Jake's on a Tuesday for lunch, chief."

"I know. I'm trying to find the right way to share with you

the depth of our depravity."

"Beaumont has its own heart of darkness. You are rather naive to believe your town is the only place with its hidden horrors. There's a blackness to every town. It worms its way out in due time, regardless of the chains we use to hold the blackness back. Did you think you alone could conceal all of your town's ugliness and shame?"

"Yes, Gallagher, I did think that way. Maybe I was the only person in Beaumont who thought our shit didn't smell."

"And now?"

"Our shit smells."

"Thought so. You know, chief, the sooner I began to believe my own shit smelled, the quicker I was able to find a way to mask it."

"I don't think there is any masking this, Gallagher."

"It all depends on what the meaning of is, is."

Louise laughed grimly and dropped some of her corned beef on her lap. She picked up a few of the larger chunks of meat and placed them in her mouth, unconsciously, like the five second rule hadn't been violated.

"So why did you call me here, chief, so cheery and all?"

"I have a problem."

"We all have problems."

"I will tell you all of this if you promise to hear me out first and let me make a decision that's best for me and my town."

"Why bring me into your decision making, then? It seems you're going to do what you are going to do."

Louise took another bite of her sandwich. She washed it down with some coffee and dabbed at her lips with her napkin. She placed it down, folding it precisely next to her plate, rearranging the silverware so they were equidistant, the fork on one side, the knife on the other. She took some sugar and poured a small amount into the remnants of her coffee, carefully stirring it with a spoon. Gallagher sat across from her and waited.

"Jack Monroe raped Mickey Cummings."

Gallagher shifted in his seat. His eyes remained fixed on Louise. He didn't look surprised.

"It was at one of Jack's travel events. Mickey was on that basketball team. He didn't have anyone to room with so he had to room with Monroe. He pinned Mickey down and raped him and then never mentioned another word to him. He showed up in Mickey's office after Mickey first got elected and claimed he had a videotape of Mickey with another man at a motel in Boston. He's blackmailing our mayor."

"Jesus."

"Mickey wants me to do nothing."

"Isn't there another trip coming up to Williamsport?"

"Yes."

"Monroe is going to hurt another kid, chief."

"Mickey wants to believe Monroe got it out of his system."

"Do you believe that Mickey was a one-off?"

"No."

"Do you think Monroe did something to Ken Richardson."

"I do now."

"You have to stop him, chief."

"Mickey says he'll kill himself if I divulge his secret. The town doesn't know Mickey is gay. It makes no fucking sense that Mickey allowed the town to give Monroe the hometown hero award."

"It makes sense knowing Mickey was blackmailed."

Louise absently stirred the spoon in her coffee.

"It most certainly does."

She put her spoon back on the table. Some of the coffee spilled onto the tabletop. She took her napkin and wiped it clean.

"OK, chief, so I think it wasn't a one-off for Monroe. I think he did the same thing to Ken Richardson and now you do too, and the hometown hero thing pushed Ken over the edge. The video Monroe has of Mickey has kept the mayor quiet. And hell, Ken left his basketball shoes behind. He knew you'd figure it out." Gallagher sat for a bit. "And your husband is tied up in this dark thing Louise. He knows something."

Louise' lip trembled slightly. She put a napkin to her face to cover it up, but Gallagher had already seen it. No one else who might have been looking at her at the time would have noticed it, but Gallagher certainly did.

"You're going to have to talk with your husband when he comes around, chief."

"I know. It will be very hard."

"Yes. Yes, it most certainly will."

The fishing was easy. Ken sat with his feet at the edge of the pond, toes dipped luxuriously into the cool water. His gold basketball shoes sat next to him on the riverbank. His father had never fished with him, so he didn't have a rod. Jack Monroe had a rod. Ken caught two sunfish and a listless carp.

"I'm hungry. Let's eat our lunch up there. Jack Monroe pointed up the slope to the path that led along the crest of the high hill, up by the rope swing. "The pond stinks." Ken took his toes out of the water. He put on his gold basketball shoes, leaving the laces untied. He climbed the hill first, Jack very close behind. They reached the top in no time. Ken used the rope hanging from the tree to pull himself up to the top. Jack dug his fingers into the bank of the hill and pulled himself upright. His hands were soiled when he stood erect. It was a very quiet afternoon in the forest during a summer that had been oppressively hot. They set out the picnic lunch and watched the river as it coursed relentlessly toward the Atlantic Ocean, some thirty miles away. It was too hot a day. No one was by the river or the pond or the rope swing, so no one noticed as they ate their lunch alone.

Chapter 25

Prawns

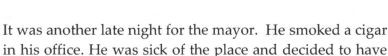

It was another late night for the mayor. He smoked a cigar in his office. He was sick of the place and decided to have dinner at the Jade. It had the best Chinese food in town, and it was late so he would be able to eat in peace. He needed to eat in peace.

His face still stung from the slap Louise Consola had given him that morning. It was deserved. Actually, he deserved so much more. But he had been honest with her. He would kill himself if she divulged his secrets.

His meal arrived. He had ordered prawns with duck sauce. They came with the shell, so Mickey tore at the exoskeleton to get at the juicy meat. He found it comforting to disembowel the prawn. He wiped his face with a cloth napkin. He was about to rip another prawn apart when he felt a presence loom up by his table. He looked up. Jack Monroe stood across from Mickey. The cuff at the legs of his khaki pants was too short, revealing a brand-new pair of black Converse All-Stars. He wanted new sneakers for his upcoming trip.

"Well, what a surprise. Hello mayor."

Mickey put down his prawn and stared at the cooked animal and his appetite disappeared. He looked up as Jack took a chair opposite from him. "Expecting someone?"

"I'm eating alone."

"Really. No one exotic meeting you here later, perhaps? Any one I would know?"

"Christ, Jack."

"I just hate to see one of my boys eating by himself. It makes me sad to think of you going home alone."

"Fuck you."

"Well, that's not very friendly, mayor."

"I have no business with you."

"You don't, mayor?"

"I don't."

"Well, I have some business with you. I wanted to show you this." Jack reached into his jacket and pulled out a black video tape. "Recognize this."

"Fuck."

"No one knows about the tape, Mickey, except you and me. But all of that can change."

Mickey felt the prawn churn in his gut. He fought against the reflex to throw up. He took two long, deep breaths and put both his hands on the table. A bead of moisture began to form on his forehead. Jack sat back in his chair. A smile formed along his thin lips. His forehead began to furrow and the elastic that held his thick glasses in place began to stretch. Mickey balled up his fists like he was going to leap across the table.

"You angry, mayor?"

"Just leave and let me eat in peace."

"I thought with everything going on, Hank's terrible accident and him being in the hospital, and poor Ken going ahead and killing himself, I thought maybe you would like a reminder. It would be a shame if this video got into the wrong hands. I'm sure the Boston stations and social media would eat it up. 'Local mayor outed.' It wouldn't be pretty for you, Mickey."

"I've kept our secret, Jack."

"And I've kept yours."

Mickey took his napkin and began to dab away the moisture that was forming along his forehead. Jack showed his shark teeth as his smile deepened. The bottom row was crooked.

"That's the reaction I wanted to see, mayor. Here, take this copy. I have many more. Watch it tonight and ask yourself what the town would say."

"You son of a bitch." Mickey stood quickly.

Jack's smile disappeared and Mickey saw the same face he saw years ago in the motel room after Jack had violated him. The face morphed into a hideous leer.

"Remember, mayor. You'll always be one of my boys."

Jack turned and walked out of the restaurant. Some busboys busied themselves clearing away dirty, crusted dishes and stained wine glasses. Mickey watched Jack walk out. The bile forming in his stomach could not be held down and he threw up on his table, mangled prawn spilling out and soiling the tablecloth. He raced from the table, out the back door and sped off into the night. The stench of puke was heavy on him as his car careened through his town. The night was black and through his tears, it was hard for Mickey to see just about anything at all as Beaumont flew past in the dead of night.

Chapter 26

Social Media

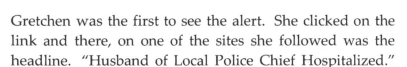

Gretchen was the first to see the alert. She clicked on the link and there, on one of the sites she followed was the headline. "Husband of Local Police Chief Hospitalized." The shock of the post horrified her.

"Reports from Mass General confirm that Hank Consola, husband of Chief Louise Consola of the Beaumont Police Department, has been admitted to the psych ward. This follows Mr. Consola's recent near-fatal car accident not long after the death of Ken Richardson, a local businessman who was found on the Fish Brook Dam in Beaumont after an apparent suicide."

The air in Gretchen's lungs rushed out and she let out a high-pitched wail that woke her sister. Pammy leaped out of her bed and rushed to Gretchen. She kneeled down on the bed and grabbed the phone from her sister. She read the article. Pammy breathed through her nose. The noise of rushing air was amplified by the closeness of the bedroom they shared. Within seconds, Gretchen's Twitter feed erupted with messages from friends and even people she did not know.

"Why was her father in a psych ward?"

"Was he mental?"

"What was wrong with him? Was he psycho?"

"Your father is nuts."

"Christ, Gretchen. We have to show this to mom."

"No we don't."

"She said we could handle it the way we wanted to, and now the story about dad is out."

"Mom said this might happen, that people might not understand and fly off the handle. She said so."

"I'm showing this to mom," Pammy said, pulling the phone out of her sister's hands.

The two girls raced to their mother's room. She sat on her bed, her own cell phone in her hand. She scrolled down and looked at one message after another about her husband's condition. She crossed her ankles and watched as her twin daughters walked into the room. They sat on their mother's bed as she looked back down to her phone. Even she was shocked at the number of shares the article had received and the ever-growing likes the page had been given. It seemed like the entire world was now aware of the fragile mental condition of Hank Consola.

Finally, having seen enough and after deleting some of the foul messages strangers had posted, anonymous, infantile strangers, she turned her phone off and looked at her daughters.

"We are so sorry, mom. We only told a few of our friends, the ones we thought we could trust."

"No, it was bound to get out, girls. I'm sure your friends didn't do this or maybe they didn't mean to do this. Some people can't seem to help themselves. Social media has stolen our souls."

The girls reached over to their mother and pulled her in close. The only sounds were the muffled sobs they shared for the man they loved at a hospital too far away.

They left the rope swing behind. Jack put his arm around Ken, his boy. A large oak loomed in front of them, toppled by a terrible storm that had passed that way not long before. It lay on its side, root ball exposed to the dying sun, exposing a deep crater, long fingers of roots holding desperately to the dank, rotting soil. The trunk of the oak had ruined that part of the forest, squashing saplings as they strained in vain for the hope of life from the distant sun, never to find their way. Jack guided Ken to the edge of the crater and they sat. His left leg rested against Ken's right. A confusion set in and Ken Richardson sat paralyzed as Jack moved a hairy hand onto Ken's knee and then down his shin, slipping off the basketball shoes and discarding them in the crater. Ken sat paralyzed as cicadas called out for each other, high in the overlooking trees.

Chapter 27

Hand Gun

Mickey Cummings sat on the stoop of Louise Consola's front porch. He had parked his car down the street and walked over in the deepest part of the night. He held the gun against his thigh. He had raised it and lowered it three times as bright stars shined down from the unforgiving, relentless heavens. Each time, he had gone so far as to cock the hammer. His trigger finger twitched only to relax when a lone fox scurried across the street. It held a struggling rabbit in its mouth. A quick snap of the jaw and the bunny was out of its misery. Mickey put the gun down and waited for the dawn. Slowly, his head sagged, and the unrelenting strain of the night overcame him. He fell forward, stumbling off the porch, landing on the front yard. The fox ran on. It needed to feed its young in a den hidden deep in the forest.

Louise opened her front door to get the morning paper. She stepped on the lawn and almost stumbled over Mickey. He lay on his side. She could smell the booze and the vomit that stained his shirt. She caught herself when she noticed the gun that lay next to Mickey's right hand. The hammer was cocked and the barrel remained pointed at Mickey's head. She stepped quickly over Mickey's prone body. She carefully picked up the gun and released the hammer. She placed it deliberately on one of the two rocking chairs that sat moist in the early morning dew. She made sure it was on the chair farthest from Mickey's prone body.

A low moan rose from him as he began to come to. He tried to sit up but his head spun from the night before. Drool hung from his bottom lip. He looked around, disoriented as the sun broke over the horizon. He tried to focus on Louise who had sat down next to him on the wet grass. She ran her hand through Mickey's matted, white hair. "It's a bit early to be stopping by, my friend." She brushed Mickey's hair back into place. "You don't look too good."

He burped a bit of verp into his throat and swallowed it down with an effort. HIs face contorted as the taste of gin and Chinese food rolled from the back of his throat down into his gut.

"You don't smell too good, either."

"Perhaps not."

"Good Lord, man. What happened to you?"

Mickey sat up, pulling his knees close to his chest. He sat silently. Birds came alive, chirping joyously, carrying on morning conversations about the prospects of another fine day. The morning began to warm and his eyes finally began to clear. "So what's with the gun, Mickey?"

He looked around, expecting the gun to be close, but Louise had moved it away. Mickey sighed and dropped his chin to his chest.

"I don't really have much to say about the gun."

"So why have it with you? You're scaring me, Mickey."

"I'm beginning to scare myself, chief." The two sat without

looking at each other.

"I won't let you kill yourself."

"I think that's probably why I ended up here, Louise. I know if I am here with you, I'm safe from him and I'm safe from myself. And you're right. Jack will do it again. I think I've known that all along, even when the town selected him as one of their heroes. We've been blind to his evil, Louise, and it has corrupted me and it has corrupted the town, even if they don't know it. Too many boys have been hurt, but again, I can't be the one who stops him. I'm not sure anyone can stop him without it revealing the ugly truth about our town. Hell, Ken carried that darkness until it consumed him. He could have said something. I could have said something."

"But no one did, and now you would have me keep the secret hidden when you now admit that the boys heading off to Williamsport are not safe from that monster."

"I think you're ignoring something, Louise. Maybe you're just too close to see it."

"Come out with it, Christ!"

"I think you're ignoring your husband and what he has to know."

The muscles on Louise' shoulders began to bunch and her face was pulled tight.

"What are you saying, Mickey?"

"I don't believe it was just Ken and me who knew about our town's monster. I think your husband knows. Think about it. His best friend is dead. They were inseparable. Ken took his secret to his grave and Hank had to bury him. Then Hank gets sick and now he's in a psych ward."

He tried to sit up straight, but he was still dizzy, and his hangover hurt his head.

"I think your husband knew that Ken was raped, and that Jack Monroe did it."

The enormousness of it bore down on her. She shuddered in the early morning heat and understood that everything Mickey was saying had to be true. Everything about Ken and Mickey and Hank and the other boys in town coalesced and she accepted the truth of all of it in the quick of the early morning dawn.

"That's what I think, Louise. Ask Hank when he comes around. I think that is what put him in the hospital. Don't be surprised by the truth of it. But remember you promised to protect me."

"How much more do you think I can bear if in fact my husband has been keeping the knowledge that there is a monster in our town, just like you have?"

"You would be protecting me, the town, and your husband. The town will die if it finds out people have known and did nothing. Your husband knew and did nothing." Mickey stood. He had to hold on to the railing of the porch to steady himself.

"You ask too much of me, Mickey. Why can't you show some courage and step forward? Tell what you know. The town will survive it."

"It will not. I swear to God it will not."

Mickey looked at the gun. He tried to force a smile. Instead his face contorted. His skin was pulled tight across his face showing bleached bones pushing their way through his stretched skin. Without saying another word, he turned away. Louise watched him walk across her front lawn, down the street to his car parked a few houses away. She sat in the chair next to the one where she had placed Mickey's gun a few minutes before. It had a dull shine in spite of the early morning light. She picked it up and checked to see if there were bullets in the chamber. It was almost fully loaded. She placed her nose next to the gun. The smell of cordite was distinct. The gun had been fired recently. She sat in horror as she realized that Mickey Cummings had failed last night to do what he had threatened he would do. She set the gun down. She stared into a pit of darkness even though the sun was beginning to climb luxuriously into the heat of a fair, Massachusetts morning.

When Ken came to, he was face down in the putrid soil of the crater. He got up on his hands and knees and looked around. The root ball loomed above him, brutal appendages dug deep into the bleak earth. He looked down. His pants were bunched at his knees. His gold Converse All-Stars lay in the muck at the bottom of the crater. He reached down and took hold of them, slipping them back on his ruined feet. His fingernails were thick with dirt from where he had dug his hands into the soil not long ago when he was driven into the earth. His backside ached from the brutality of it. He stood up and instinctively, let out a scream as he tried to pull himself out of the crater. No one was anywhere near to hear him howl in

fear, and what would he say if someone came to his rescue? He pulled himself out of the crater and looked around to see if his coach was near. He must have left, how long ago Ken did not know.

He walked back toward the rope swing and the bank overlooking the pond and the dam and the mostly dead river. The sun was setting as he set off in the direction of his neighborhood, down a path he thought he used to know but had changed enough that he didn't recognize it anymore. He became disoriented until he saw a familiar rock jutting from the soil, hard by a twist to the path. Now he knew where he was and didn't at the same time.

He tried to breathe but he could not get enough air into his lungs. He tried to scream, again, and this time no sound came out. He tried again and then, again, once more. There was nothing left inside to come out of him, a hollowed-out boy. He looked about his favorite woods. The trees cast merciless shadows as he headed back home through the twisted paths of the darkening forest, never to be who he was again. He dragged his feet, soiling his gold basketball shoes, stained by the muck and grime of the hideous paths.

Chapter 28

Awakening

The girls slept painfully on uncomfortable chairs in their father's hospital room. They woke, stretching their backs and trying to get the kinks out of their necks. Louise walked back and forth at the end of the bed. She was on the phone with Betty, making sure things in town were quiet. Betty told her that everything was fine and not to worry. She told Louise that the only thing was that the town continued to buzz over Hank's hospitalization. The idiots in town seemed to be feasting on the notion that the husband of the chief of police was mentally ill.

"Jesus, how ignorant can people be, Betty?"

"Apparently very, chief."

"I don't get it, and I never will. It sickens me."

"Everything passes over time, chief. This will all blow over and we can get back to normal."

"Normal. What if our normal was corrupted and we didn't know it?"

"Chief?"

Louise was about to say more when she noticed Hank begin to stir in his bed. He shifted from his right side to his left and opened his eyes. "Hank just woke up, Betty. I'll call you back."

She hung up her phone and moved quickly to her husband's side. Hank's eyes cleared and he focused on his wife's face. He reached out. An IV was fastened to the back of his hand. It was badly bruised from the many times he had pulled the IV out as he thrashed in bed, unconscious in his nightmares. The nurses had struggled to keep the IV in place. Louise touched his hand gently and leaned forward to kiss her husband,

"Hello, stranger. It's good to have you back."

"Where am I?"

Pammy and Gretchen stepped quickly around the bed and rested their heads on their father's chest. They cried quietly. Hank ran his hands through his daughters' hair. He looked around.

"I'm in a hospital."

"Yes, you've been here for a couple of days."

"And you've been here too?"

"Yes. Betty came in once or twice. Gallagher too. And Mickey Cummings."

"Mickey was here?"

"Yes. I had to send him home. He wouldn't leave. I told him he still had a town to run."

She laughed as the girls sat up and moved back to their chairs. They cried quietly now that their father was back.

"Louise, I'm so sorry. I've put you and the girls through too much."

He looked up at the ceiling and began to cry. Louise and the twins sat and watched their father. They swallowed hard, trying to control themselves as they watched his emotions laid bare. He took a deep breath and gathered himself. It was a strain but he regained control.

"Girls, can you give me some time alone with your mother?"

"Can't we stay? We've missed you."

"Please."

"Come on Pammy, we'll get some lunch. Do you want anything?"

"Perhaps later."

"Sure, daddy."

Louise stood up and walked to the door with her daughters. She kissed them both and held them tightly.

"Daddy's back."

Pammy and Gretchen and Louise touched foreheads together and breathed deeply, probably for the first time since their father had become ill.

"He probably still has a long way to go."

Louise bowed her head and began to pray.

"Dear God, thank you for the gift of giving us back my husband and the father of our girls. We ask in your name that you bring him back to health and let him heal. In your name we pray. Amen."

They remained with their heads touching for a few moments. When they were able to breathe properly, now that it seemed their father was going to be ok, Pammy and

Gretchen walked down the hallway toward the elevators. They waited for the doors to open, holding hands quietly as other families waited with them. A bell rang and the doors opened. Louise watched her twins disappear with a small crowd as the elevator doors opened. Pammy and Gretchen walked into the elevator with the rest of the people. The doors closed and she found herself in the hallway by herself. A lone nurse walked down the hall, swiping through an iPad checking on the condition of other patients. Louise turned back into the room and looked at her husband. He had watched his family pray for him.

"Thank you for that, Louise."

She pulled up a chair and sat next to her husband's bed.

"Why don't you close your eyes and rest? I'm not going anywhere. I'll be here for as long as it takes. I thought I had lost you, Hank."

"I'm so sorry, but I don't want to go back to sleep. Please, I have things I need to say."

Louise sat in her chair and waited for her husband.

"There is something you should know. I've kept it buried for too long. I thought I could keep it there, hidden deep. But Ken died and it almost shattered me." He looked at his wife for a bit, taking two quick, shallow breaths. "I don't think Ken had to kill himself. I think he was driven to do it. I think it was a murder, Louise."

"I don't understand. He made a video and I watched him die."

"Have you asked yourself why?"

"That's all I've asked since he passed away. He was my friend too,"

"But he died on that one day, the day Jack Monroe became a hometown hero. It was too much for him."

He looked at his wife. His fists began to ball and his jaw clenched. It took all of his effort to continue on, to let the beast out and still maintain control over it.

"I told you it was my fault. I could have saved him."

Louise looked at her husband. She knew that a blackened truth was oozing out and she waited to meet the beast for herself.

"I've known for years. I've known about Jack Monroe and I've known what he has done to little boys, what he tried to do to me, what he was able to do to Ken." Hank closed his eyes tight and beat the animal back. "He raped him when he was a little boy. Ken told me and he made me swear to tell no one, but now Ken's gone, and our town has made Jack a hero."

Louise stood up and began to pace back and forth. She held her hands together and then pulled them apart suddenly, like they burned and were torture to keep together. After a moment, she sat back down.

"I know. Mickey told me that you probably knew about Jack. Christ, this is ugly. You see, Mickey was raped by Jack too. The three of you. You've all been ruined, and Mickey has made me promise to keep his secret. He says the town would never accept the truth. And now my husband tells me he has known about Jack for years. What will happen to you and Mickey if I arrest Jack? It would destroy you and

Mickey, me, the girls, everyone. How can I protect the town from the monster we let live in our midst? How can I protect you and Mickey?"

"You mean the animal that I let live in our midst. I told you it was my fault. But there is more. Louise, being honest now, I have to say that the overwhelming emotion at the time, the one that stayed with me most powerfully, wasn't that Ken was raped. What was more important to me, the thing I realize now, the real beast I've held at bay, is that I was simply relieved that it wasn't me."

"My God, you were just a boy. What could you have done at the time?"

"But I knew he was a monster. I knew it after the first time he took Ken and me to that first Celtic's game. I knew it and it petrified me, and I could have said something to Ken, but I didn't. I let him get raped."

"You can't do that to yourself, Hank."

"But it's true. That monster didn't get me, and at the time, that was what mattered, although I'm sure I couldn't articulate it then. I'm ashamed of it. I don't know if I will ever find a way to forgive myself for it."

Louise felt her heart pounding in her chest, accepting the truth to what her husband was sharing, wondering too if he could ever be able to forgive himself. She bowed her head and tried to plow ahead.

"There's more, Hank. Jack cut your brake lines. He tried to kill you. Mickey told me Jack is blackmailing him to keep quiet. He has another trip to Williamsport coming up. Someone else is going to be hurt, Hank. I have to do something, but whatever I do will hurt you and Mickey and the town."

"I don't know what to say. I really don't."

"My God, Hank. I don't see an end to this without me sacrificing you and Mickey."

"It has to stop, chief."

"Nothing is as simple as just having to stop. I don't think there is any way out of this, Hank. I don't. I just see this evil ravaging Beaumont and I'm the chief of police and impotent as hell. I hate knowing it. Christ, I hate that man, and I've never hated anyone, ever."

"If you don't do something, Jack is going to hurt someone again. He's probably been doing it for years. How many kids have to be sacrificed for the reputation of our fucking town?"

"I won't destroy you or Mickey or Ken's memory. I won't do it. I can't do it."

"I know, and that is the problem."

The two sat in the quiet of the hospital and they heard nothing of the silent anguish from other families that hung in the air.

The two boys sat on a picnic table behind Ken's house. His mother sat on the porch with a drink in one hand and a cigarette in the other. His dad was away, again, making money on a different coast, believing that the money that he took in made up

for his time away. It didn't, not to Ken. He was twelve now, almost a full year since the afternoon at the root ball and the crater, down by the river, when his soul was stolen and his childhood ended. Without warning, he began to sob. Hank looked startled at his friend, who never cried, no matter what, ever.

"Hank, can I tell you something? Please? Promise me you'll tell no one." Ken's mother took a long drag from her cigarette and looked across the neighborhood. She heard nothing of what her lovely, fractured boy said on that hot, summer afternoon.

Chapter 29

Louisville Slugger

Tommy Timmons entered Whitford's Sporting Goods with his dad. He wanted to buy a new bat. He had his heart set on the new, Louisville Slugger "20-20 Prime". His dad said it was too much, but Tommy Timmons persisted. Coach Monroe had promised him more playing time next year, and since the team would be playing plenty of pick-up games at Williamsport, he wanted to make a good impression on his coach. His dad relented and paid the $400. He was like most fathers and mothers. No price was too high to pay for the love they had for their children.

Louise sat in her office during the busiest time of the day. Shifts were changing and she needed to oversee the traffic of officers moving through the station. Things began to settle down as Gallagher walked in. He sat in a chair across from Louise. She took a sip from a bottle of water.

"Want some?"

"Please."

She stood up and walked to a small refrigerator in the corner of her office. She pulled out the coldest bottle she could find and handed it to Gallagher. He took his large hands and easily screwed off the top. He took a long drink as Louise sat back down at her desk.

"I heard Hank's home."

"Thank God."

"Have you two talked?"

"We have."

Gallagher sat and waited. He took another long pull from the water bottle. He kept his eyes on Louise. She didn't seem inclined to speak.

"Do you have anything you'd like to share with me, chief?"

"No."

"Christ, Louise. I come here on my time off. I'm trying to help with whatever stinks in this town, because something indeed does stink in lovely Beaumont."

Louise folded her hands and said nothing. He continued to sit, hoping to wait her out until whatever stunk up the town would spill out. They sat for five long minutes, measuring each other's breathing, the tension in the air as thick as the oppressive humidity that draped over the town. She couldn't say anything and she knew it. Still, she felt like she was looking into the abyss and anything she might say would loosen her tenuous foothold and she would fall and die well before she hit the bottom.

Looking frustrated, Gallagher was about to get up and leave when Betty burst into the office.

"Chief, it's the mayor."

"I promise. I promise to the day I die. I swear, Ken. Please stop

crying. I promise, I promise, I promise. I'll never say a word." Hank put his hand on Ken's shoulder. Ken's mom took another long drag from her cigarette. A thin blue line of smoke escaped from her lipsticked mouth and once more, she took a sip from her martini glass.

Chapter 30

Best-Dressed Man

Louise and Gallagher followed behind Betty as they turned onto the road where Mickey Cummings lived. There was another cruiser parked in front and an ambulance idled in the mayor's driveway. An unfamiliar car was parked next to the ambulance.

Betty stepped out of her cruiser quickly and entered Mickey's home. The door was open. A pane of glass had been broken and a rock lay on the kitchen floor. Gallagher and Louise followed close behind. After Gallagher entered the house, Louise stopped short of the doorway between the mudroom and Mickey's kitchen. She willed herself to step across the threshold and into the kitchen where she had visited Mickey that very early morning just a few days before. She could see a stretcher in the solarium. This time, the sun was on the other side of the house and the solarium was dark. Louise felt a wave of nausea. She steadied herself in the kitchen before stepping inside.

The bamboo plants stood erect in their pots. The solarium was spotless, except for a stain on the oriental rug, directly under the lifeless form of Mickey Cummings as he hung from a rope strung from a rafter. He wore a beautiful blue blazer over a starched, button-down shirt, His gold tie hung down from his neck, a perfect roll in his collar. It was clasped near his waist by a shining, gold tie-clip with blue edges, the colors of Beaumont. He wore perfectly ironed, pleated grey slacks and polished, wing-tip shoes with a hint of burgundy. His perfectly white hair was brushed back expertly. It was long and wavy and distinguished in a way Louise had seen many times when Mickey had presided over some political affair or expensive banquet.

A man sat on the rug. He held his head in his hands and cried softly.

"We were supposed to have lunch today. When he didn't show, I called his cell and he didn't answer. I came right over. The front door was locked. I came around back and looked into the solarium. That's when I saw Mickey. I threw a rock through the glass in the front door so I could get in. I thought I could save him. But he was gone already. I called 9-1-1. My God, why would he do this? He was such a wonderful, beautiful man."

Betty helped the man up and led him out of the solarium. He held his face to his hands and cried as Betty put her arm around him and helped him leave the house.

The EMTs untied the rope and carefully helped Mickey's body to the stretcher. Louise noticed they were the same EMTs from the dam when Ken had been found.

"We're so sorry, chief," they said as she entered the solarium and stood next to the stretcher.

Gallagher took a pair of rubber gloves out of his coat pocket. One of the EMTs gave him an olive-green towel which Gallagher used to clean up the stain underneath where Mickey had killed himself. Louise took her right hand and bending down, ran her fingers through Mickey's silver hair.

"Be finally at peace, Mickey Cummings."

She kissed him gently on his forehead and ran her fingers through his hair. She straightened up and the EMTs rolled the stretcher through the solarium and out the front door. They placed Mickey's body gently into the ambulance. One of the EMTs stepped inside with Mickey's body while the other one climbed into the driver's seat. Some neighbors had gathered and watched as the soundless ambulance drove away from Mickey's home. A lone coyote stood and watched silently from the forest. Birds that perched on power lines seemed to bow as the mayor was driven away. The sun began to set and cast a halo around the ambulance as it drove off slowly, toward the hospital.

Chapter 31

Wake

Hank sat at the kitchen table. Cold meat loaf sat on his plate. The girls sat next to their father. They picked at their mashed potatoes. Louise looked out the window to her backyard. Her chest felt tight all day and now her blood pulsed painfully through the arteries leading up the side of her neck. Her head pounded and she rubbed her fingers against her temples. She hadn't cried since Mickey died. She didn't think she had any tears to shed. Her mind was haunted by the idea that another life was over and Jack Monroe was directly responsible, even as she knew she could not let the truth out. The press had asked questions, of course. They always did, the prying bastards. She had said only that Mickey's death was a great tragedy and everyone should respect his privacy.

She was paralyzed by the reality that Jack Monroe was a few days away from his next trip to Williamsport. She had looked at the list of boys who would be making the annual trip. She knew many of the families and even some of the boys. She looked down the list at their ages, mostly twelve and eleven-year-olds, but one ten-year-old.

Tommy Timmons was the smallest and youngest player on Jack's team. A picture crystallized in her mind of a future where Tommy was found hanging from a rafter or a bullet to his head after years of torment from being assaulted by

Jack Monroe. She suddenly felt sick. She jumped from the table and raced upstairs to her bathroom. Her stomach lurched and she dry-heaved for what seemed like an impossible time. When she finally felt there was nothing left in her gut, she reached for a towel and wiped the bile from her face. She sat back on her heels and let herself slide against the wall of her bathroom. It was cool and brought a bit of false relief. The door opened and Hank stepped in. He sat down on the floor next to his wife. He put his arm around her and pulled her close, in spite of the heavy stench of throw up.

Finally, mercifully, Chief Louise Consola broke down. She began to wail, punching her husband's chest as the grief and the horror overwhelmed her. Hank held onto his wife. He had no words for her. What was he supposed to say knowing that Ken's death was at least partly his doing and now Mickey was dead because the truth of being raped by fucking Jack Monroe was a cancer of a disease that would not relent?

"Who else is going to be destroyed, Hank?" She turned and looked at her husband. "Two men raped, you targeted, and God knows how many others. And I can't do anything."

"No, I don't think you really can."

"And who else will we have to bury?"

"Maybe no one else."

"Do you believe that?"

"No, no I don't chief."

Louise' legs splayed out on the floor. She saw no way out of her hell and the hell of her town, and a piece of her heart blackened at the thought of it all, hardening as she tried to hold on to whatever good she knew of her world.

Mickey's wake was attended by thousands. The streets around the funeral home had to be closed down because of the overwhelming traffic. Shuttle buses from the high school ferried mourners to the funeral home to lessen the traffic. Mickey's family stood dutifully as one state dignitary after another paid their respects. Entire families waited in line for hours. They spoke quietly to one another, sharing stories of Mickey's generosity and kindness. Louise and Hank and the girls made their way through the line until finally they stood in front of Mickey's open casket. All four of them kneeled and prayed for Mickey's soul. When it came time for Louise to stand in front of Mickey's mother, she felt like she might not hold it together. Hank kept his arms around his wife.

"He loved you, you know. He told me that no matter what, he could trust you." Mickey's mom leaned in close and whispered so that only Louise could hear. "He told me that you were the one person he knew could keep his secret. God bless you for that, Louise."

"Thank you, Mrs. Cummings. I could have done more."

"You do what you need to do in this life, Louise. Never forget that."

Louise bowed her head and said nothing. Mrs. Cumming's words ripped out a piece of her heart. Her shoulders began to shake in spite of her best efforts. Mrs. Cummings held Louise close and the two of them cried together. The line behind them began. Hank guided his wife and the girls away. Louise ignored some of the people who sat in chairs or milled about. She needed to be away from the abject pain of the place. The Consola family walked out the back door and down the street to the police station where Louise had parked her cruiser. They drove home in silence. Neither Hank nor Louise so much as glanced at each other. They were in the middle of their private pain, one that they could not speak of and certainly, could never let the girls know of the awfulness they held between themselves. The girls rode in silence and never once used their cell phones.

Later that night, she and Hank held each other in the dark of their bedroom. There was no moon that night and the stars were exceptionally and surprisingly bright. She disengaged from her husband and stepped out onto the porch just outside their bedroom. Hank joined her a few minutes later. He handed her a glass of wine. They drank together, barely holding in the overwhelming emotions that bore down on them.

"Are you going to the funeral, Hank? Maybe it will be too much. You've only just gotten out of the hospital."

"Of course, I am."

"It will be hard."

"Yes."

Hank took a second sip from his wine glass. Louise looked up at the black, cloudless night. She could see the edge of the Milky Way and the billions of systems that swirled about the endlessness of the universe.

"God has Mickey now," she said as a slight breeze moved her hair across her forehead.

"And what about us, Louise? Will God ever forgive us?"

"I don't think so."

Louise set her wine glass down on the railing of their porch. She put her hand on her husband's shoulder and then walked back into their bedroom. She pulled the covers tight over her in spite of the summer's heat. Hank joined her moments later. He spooned against her and stroked her hair. The room remained dark as the two eventually drifted off into a sleep filled with fitful dreams.

Chapter 32

Shovels of Dirt

Louise and Hank stood in the row directly behind the Cummings family. She could see that Gallagher sat in one of the folding chairs set up for the people who came to bury Mickey. A minister said some words in a futile attempt to comfort the friends and family in attendance. She heard none of those words. They were empty to her now.

She stood shocked at the scene that was unfolding before her. There, sitting in the back row, next to Tommy Timmons and his father, sat Jack Monroe. He wore an old suit that perhaps fit him well twenty years ago, but now, it strained at the shoulders and bunched by his hips. The shirt he wore bulged at his waist. The sun was in his face, so he had his hand up, concealing whatever evil danced behind his thick glasses and lifeless eyes. Louise held her breath. Hank sensed the change in his wife.

"What is it?" he whispered.

"Jack Monroe is here."

Hank's grip tightened on Louise' shoulders. They stared at the man, the sun behind them so he could not see the venomous hate that blanched their faces. They watched in horror as Monroe put his arm around the back of Tommy's chair. His father's eyes were also blinded by the light from behind the casket, so maybe he didn't notice Jack's arm or maybe he didn't see the problem with it. Hank began to inch away from Louise like he was trying to get at Jack. She held his arm and kept him in place. He stiffened against her hand, but held his spot. She could hear his breath labor and his heart beat hard though his black suit.

When the service ended, Louise and Hank helped take small shovels of dirt, dropping earth on Mickey's casket. The top of it slowly began to be covered until finally, everyone who was going to place earth on Mickey's casket had finished doing so.

Slowly, the crowd began to disperse. Gallagher stood up from his chair and looked around at the people in attendance. He saw Jack Monroe shaking hands with first Mr. Timmons and then Tommy. Something dark broke through, and in spite of the self-control cultivated in him by years of time on the state police force, he found himself striding toward Monroe. As Jack walked away with Mr. Timmons and his son, Gallagher drew even. Jack didn't notice Gallagher moving alongside him. Gallagher took the thumb from his meaty right hand and jabbed it against Jack's ribs. He increased the pressure until Jack felt a bolt of excruciating pain. His body contorted, turning quickly away from Gallagher.

"I beg your pardon. I didn't mean to bump into you," Gallagher said apologetically.

"Jesus!" Jack grabbed at his ribs and let out a yelp.

In the intense sunlight of the day, he did not recognize Gallagher. Quickly, Gallagher turned away, into the sunlight, and walked off before Jack could recognize him. He felt a perverse sense of satisfaction inflicting pain on Monroe, the hometown hero. As he walked back toward the burial site, he saw that Louise and Hank were standing there and had witnessed the entire incident. When he reached them, he said nothing, but the look on his face showed that he was pleased with his clandestine act. They walked away, the three of them, feeling that whatever had just transpired between Gallagher and Monroe could never come close to the level of retribution the man deserved.

They sat at a bar in the afternoon, not long after Mickey's burial. Hank and Gallagher drank scotch while Louise nursed a beer. They drank in silence. The waitress kept her distance. She could sense a palpable anger in the booth where they sat. Finally, Gallagher spoke.

"I should have let him alone."

"I'm glad you did what you did, Gallagher," Hank spoke softly as he downed the rest of his scotch. "I might not have been able to control myself if I had stood as close as you to that prick."

"You should have left him alone, Gallagher. The man is a monster. We know what he can do, what he will do. He tried to kill Hank. Don't push him."

"Christ, Louise," Gallagher let out slowly. "I don't know what I'd do in your situation but keeping quiet will not be the answer. What are you protecting him for? He deserves nothing."

"I'm not protecting the man. I'm protecting my husband and the memory of the mayor."

Louise became agitated, letting out something that she had been considering but hadn't yet voiced.

"Do you think these are the only two men who have kept the secret depravity of Jack Monroe? How many other men walk the streets of Beaumont having been victimized by the bastard? Where have they been, can you please tell me that? What have they done to put a stop to it? Why do I have to be the one to step up to the plate? I'm this man's wife and I will not betray him!"

She found her voice raised enough that a few people at the bar turned to look but quickly spun back on their barstools when they realized it was the chief of police making a scene.

"Louise!" Hank blurted out.

She lowered her voice but the venom of her emotions could not be contained.

"No, Hank!" she whispered harshly, trying to contain her anger. "What kind of a town do we have when kids are sacrificed to protect the adults and the reputation of our little piece of suburbia? I've fucking had it with this place."

She grabbed her beer mug and drained it. She wiped the foam off of her lips and placed the mug carefully on the table, trying desperately to control her emotions. The lightness of the mug being placed on the table did nothing to reduce the intensity of the stillness in the booth. No one spoke. Louise looked down at her beer. Hank held his empty scotch glass near his mouth. Gallagher coughed quietly and spoke. He put his hands up, making two stop signs.

"Chief, too many towns have a Jack Monroe. Your town is like too many I've been in. It would have to admit to the evil of itself. Most towns don't want to go through that kind of introspection. What kind of blindness must a town cling to until it begins to see the light of day? Don't be so hard on yourselves. Most towns will never face the realities of their own monsters. Maybe the best we can do is accept that they exist and minimize the carnage."

Their throats tightened as they sat in silence. Cars drove down Main Street and people came into the bar or left it, walking quickly outside. The late afternoon sun baked them all as they scurried on their way to find shade from the searing heat.

Chapter 33

Root Ball Crater

There was one day to go before Jack was set to take his team to Williamsport. In spite of the loss of the town's beloved mayor, the kids on the team and their parents were giddy over the upcoming trip and all that Coach Monroe had planned for the boys. Bags were already packed, new baseball equipment was purchased, and contact information was exchanged. Most parents planned on driving the six hours to Central Pennsylvania to witness the festivities, even though they would have to spend their nights at a different hotel from the one Jack had booked for him and his boys. That was fine with the parents, though. They knew their sons were in the best of hands.

Louise parked her cruiser next to the water treatment plant, hard against the dam that separated Fish Brook from the almost lifeless Merrimack River. She made her way onto the dam. Two dead carp floated belly-up at its base. A raccoon had made its way to where the dead fish rotted in the swill of the river. It ignored Louise, ripping off pieces of the dead fish, licking sticky blood from its mauling paws. Louise almost lost her balance as she passed near the raccoon. She caught herself and cursed, loud enough to startle two crows that perched high on a tree that bent over the river. They flew off in protest. The loudness of their cawing bothered other birds nearby who also took wing. It was early in the morning. A dense fog hung over the middle of the river and except for the noise of the river lapping against the dam and the dead fish bobbing about, the area was blanketed in a quiet mist. It was loud with a stillness that echoed across the valley.

Louise stepped off the dam and began to climb up the steep hill. The rope swing hung motionless as she reached the top. She remained bent over until she forced air back into her lungs. She glanced to her left and spied the same rock where Ken had placed his cell phone perfectly so it could record his final moments. She looked down to where Ken's body lay not too many weeks earlier. The image remained vivid in her memory. She knew that there was no pulling it back and she would carry the horror of it forever. Too many assholes had shared or retweeted his bloated image. It was the way of social media to share such humiliating and disgusting pictures, and she knew that there was absolutely nothing that could be done to put that genie back in its disgusting bottle. Social media had permanently disemboweled the soul of her country. It added to the brutality of the world and it sickened her. So much sickened her.

She turned and began a slow walk along the running path. The early morning revealed the fallen oak and the upended root ball. She stepped closer and looked down into the crater left behind when that magnificent tree had given up its claim to the earth. The bottom of the crater was veiled in early morning shadow. Carefully, she lowered herself down into the blackest part of the hole, a grave for dead leaves and broken roots. She looked up to the rim of the crater. How easily she was concealed from anyone that might have passed by. She let out a loud yell. The noise of it was engulfed by the blackness and the deadness of the hole.

She thought of Ken's grave, and now Mickey Cumming's. And then she began to imagine a young boy, pinned down in this black pit with no one to see him struggle or anyone to hear his muffled cries. She thought of all the times Ken had spent with her family at cookouts and pizza parties, soccer games and birthdays. And now, with the gift of time and memory cleared of confusion and misinterpretations, she began to realize how his subdued nature was clearly mistaken for something so very different. He had been victimized by pure evil and had carried it right up to the time the town decided to honor the man who had raped him so many years earlier.

Monroe's honor was a second rape for Ken, she knew, and she agonized over the callousness of a town that could discard one of its own so easily, even if it was ignorant of its sin. And her husband knew of the rape and Mickey suspected as much and even had been raped himself. Ken and Mickey held the secret of their town's monster, literally to their graves. Louise knew the truth of all of it and as she stood there in the pit, she tried to internalize the pain Ken and Mickey carried, even what her husband carried. Her legs weakened and she found it almost impossible to hold herself up, like she would somehow be swallowed by the evil of that place.

The sun began to climb over the forest on the other side of the river. A ray of light broke through the trees. It blinded her and she quickly moved her hand to shield her eyes, and what became clear to her, the chief of police of the Town of Beaumont, Massachusetts, was that there was nothing on this God's earth that could possibly stop this monster from destroying the lives of more innocent children and their families. It was an inevitability, cold in its perfect truth.

She tried to gather her strength and overcome the realization of it all. Somehow, summoning all of her strength, she climbed out of the pit and straightened up as the full dawn broke. She began to walk, unsteadily, back towards the rope swing. As she got closer, she saw that two young boys, no older than ten, had ridden through the forest and leaned their bikes against a tree not far from the swing. Two baseball gloves lay next to their bikes. The youngest of the two took hold of the rope swing, and egged on by his friend, stepped back before racing to the edge of the hill and launching himself into the morning. At the apex of his swing, he let go and after hesitating in midair, plummeted into the pond at the terminus of Fish Brook and the innocence of the deep pond. His friend shouted out as the young boy swam back to the surface. She watched their blissful play and wondered about the uncertainty of their futures. The boy left on top of the hill didn't notice her as she stepped past him and eased herself down the steep bank. She retraced her steps along the dam. The raccoon was long gone and only the tail of the carp floated by the concrete. She reached her cruiser as the sun angled toward its zenith. Before she opened the door to leave, she looked back across the pond. The two young boys frolicked about, getting in a quick swim before they played baseball later in the day. She wondered who their coach was and whether their parents knew everything they needed to know about the man. She shook her head and with a painful sigh, she slid into the cruiser. She turned the key and the engine struggled for life like a wounded beast. She pushed on the gas and the cruiser labored up the steep hill and away from the stench of the dying river.

Later that night, after her workday was done, Louise joined her husband at the dinner table. The girls were visiting friends and said they wouldn't be home until late. The house was very quiet.

"I think I should come clean about what I knew about Ken, Louise. Keeping the secret has almost killed me. It's time the truth came out." Hank sat across the kitchen table from Louise. They held warm cups of coffee. Louise took a small sip and put her mug down on the table. She waited a few moments before she looked back up at her husband.

"No. No, not now, not after all of this time, not after Mickey killed himself."

"Christ, someone has to stop the animal."

"It's not going to be you, and think about it for a minute. What will happen to the girls if the town finds out their father knew all along that Jack raped Ken, and Mickey, and shit, even tried to get at you?"

Hank looked at his wife. She met his gaze and held it for a few moments until finally he looked back down at his mug.

"I can't stay quiet."

"You will. I'm not fighting you on this Hank. You'd be destroying yourself and the girls and me. I hate everything about this fucking situation, but that doesn't mean we have our lives ruined too."

"Our lives aren't already ruined?"

"Not like they would be if the truth came out."

"And the boys this weekend, and Tommy Timmons?"

"Don't you dare throw that in my face! Don't you dare. You don't think I understand what's at stake? Don't you fucking dare!"

Louise stood up and in the quickest of motions, slammed her mug down on the kitchen floor. The mug exploded. Shards of porcelain flew across the kitchen. Black coffee sprayed everywhere, like blood splatter at a shooting.

Hank sat quietly at the table, the noise of the broken mug still shrill in his ears. He took a deep breath before he got up. He walked to a small closet next to the refrigerator. He opened it and took out a broom. There was an old towel hanging on a hook in the closet. He took that too and walking slowly toward the kitchen table, he squatted down and began to try to clean up the mess. Louise sat back down and watched her husband try to mop up the splattered coffee and pick up the broken cup without cutting himself. She waited until he was finished before she spoke.

"We have no way out of this, Hank. I don't see one, not unless we destroy ourselves and Mickey's legacy gets ruined. We're the only ones who know he was raped, and even that he was gay for that matter, and I'm not going to betray him now that he is in the grave. I'm not."

"I know. I know, and you're right, there might not be a way out of this, ever. We are going to have to take it to our own graves, just like Ken, just like Mickey. We're already destroyed because of it. We're just going to have to live and die with all of it."

They sat by themselves in the quiet of their kitchen. They had nothing else to say. Beaumont carried on, parents driving to work and making money and having picnics and planning trips, watching baseball games and cooking steaks, drinking wine and sharing beers, swimming in pools and riding bikes in the forest, oblivious and content in its own ignorance.

Chapter 34

Gethsemane

It was getting on in the evening. Jack's trip would begin the next morning. Hank had already fallen asleep after taking a sedative the doctor had prescribed. He lay on his side with his legs stretched off of the bed, like he always did when he slept. Louise lay next to her husband. Sleep eluded her, a slippery thing too far away for her to grasp.

A growing dread had been forming in her heart as the night dragged on. She swung her legs off the side of the bed and stood up. She walked out onto her porch and sat on one of the deck chairs that she shared with her husband. She put her feet up on the railing to the porch. It was cold to the touch and she quickly pulled them off. She folded her arms against her chest and tried to separate out all of the emotions and awful truths that she held onto and the brutality and the reality to it all. Her heart began to race. Her breathing quickened in the dark. Her mouth became dry as the singular, elusive thought began to crystallize, the one that gnawed on the edges of her mind and soul. The enormousness of the situation began to coalesce into a desperate conclusion.

Two coyotes trotted nearby. They nuzzled each other as they left the openness of the backyard and plunged into the deep black of the woods that surrounded her house. Louise waited for them to return, but they never did. They were lost to the darkness, on business of their own.

She stood slowly. One cloud moved across the nighttime sky, for just a moment covering the stars with a quick shadow. She waited for the cloud to pass and the light from the stars to be revealed. A breeze quickened and the cloud moved off to cover someone else's stars.

She stepped back into the darkness of her bedroom. Hank snored mercifully, sleeping soundly for the first time in weeks. He had no more symptoms from his concussion and the cast on his arm had been removed that day. She smiled for the first time in a bit, knowing that her husband was no longer in any more physical pain. A relief, that.

She quietly stepped into her closet. She took off her nightgown and changed out of her underwear. She reached for a pair of black sweatpants and a dark, grey hoodie. She stepped out of her closet and carefully opened up her dresser drawer. She pulled out some underwear and a pair of socks. She put everything on quickly, making sure not to bump into anything that might rouse her husband. What she needed to do, what she felt compelled to do, could not be changed now and her husband waking at that moment would become an obstacle to the purposefulness of the night.

She put on a pair of running shoes that rested next to the door to her closet. She tied them quickly. She took one last look at her husband before she found herself getting down on her knees at the end of their bed. She bowed her head and began to pray. Her body shuddered as she reached out to an elusive God.

Time passed as her prayer went on. She felt an agony that

she had never felt possible. The pain of her prayer buckled her knees. She held onto the covers of her bed, desperately, hanging on so she wouldn't falter and fall to the floor. It felt like beads of warm blood coursed down her face. She tasted the blood, hot in her mouth. It was real to her in the depth of her endless despair. Still, she prayed on.

"Father, if it is your will, let this cup pass me by."

She took the back of her arm and using her hoodie, mopped away the blood she was sure streamed down her face. Her prayers went unanswered. She was fully and irrevocably separated from her God. Her soul was lost and she didn't believe she could ever be forgiven. She was sure, in fact, sure that she would never be. There would be no resurrection for her. She saw herself laid within a grotto where she was willing to sleep, a cave hidden by a stone that would never be rolled away by anyone's angels.

She pulled herself up and walked over to where her husband slept. She kissed him, gently, careful not to wake him. His body lay peacefully on the bed they shared for all these years.

She moved quickly through the darkness, past her children's room. She opened the door slowly. Both girls were fast asleep. Their cell phones sat on night tables, silenced before they fell asleep. She looked at their innocent, angelic faces and wondered what kind of hell they would face when they grew up. She didn't know everything, but she knew that they would face more turmoil, and she hoped they would be strong enough to survive whatever Sisyphean mountain they would have to climb.

She stepped lightly down the stairs. She stopped by the kitchen table and bent over, looking at the safe where her service revolver was stored, as well as the gun she and Hank kept, just in case. She thought about the gun and how it fit Hank's hand much better than hers. It was clumsy for her to hold or wield at the shooting range. She thought about it some more and then made up her mind. The gun would have to remain locked in the safe.

She took a deep breath and opened the front door. She stepped outside into the oppressive humidity of the night. The heat had been building all week and the stars were beginning to be veiled by hurrying clouds. The threat of storm was heavy on Beaumont as she leaned over and touched her toes to stretch, an odd thought on such a black night. After a few moments, she began to run down the street. She checked her watch. It was not yet midnight. She moved off at a steady pace. Her lungs worked to get enough air. She tried to keep her breathing quiet as she ran through her neighborhood and turned onto Main Street. After a mile or so, her legs began to loosen and her breathing steadied. She had three miles to run before she reached her destination.

Her pace was very quick as she drew near. She stopped at the end of the street and waited to catch her breath. When she was fully recovered, she looked up into a brooding, watchful night.

Chapter 35

Deep End

So it began. She could see a light in the backyard. She crouched down, moving stealthily along a stand of trees that surrounded the house. She stepped onto the driveway. She stopped and looked around in the gloom. The house stood alone, at least a mile from the nearest dwelling. She moved carefully now, keeping her body tight against the side of the house. When she reached the edge, she squatted down and peered into the backyard. A single light illuminated the pool. She slid along the back of the house. The floodlight was directly above her. She could not be seen from the pool because of the floodlight's singular, piercing beam. She took a deep breath, muffled it as much as possible and moved quickly toward the pool. A thief in the night.

Six beer bottles sat empty on a table not far from the water. She edged closer until she was less than a foot away from the pool. He floated on an inflatable raft, smartphone buds in his ears. He propped his phone up against his bare chest. From behind him, she looked at the oversized screen. A man stood over a boy. She felt her stomach contract and her undigested dinner begin to churn. It took all of her willpower to stifle the reflex. Slowly, she eased herself into the pool, careful to not make a sound. She moved silently through the water, doing so without making a single wave. It had to be incremental, and she made it so. She was unaware of her breathing as she inched ever closer. The night had become even darker as storm clouds formed above. A faint light pulsed off in the distance and slowly a low rumble of thunder moved over the thickness of the surrounding forest. It was too faint for him to notice with the floodlight's shine and his earbuds stuck deep. She was within inches now, fully and completely outside of herself, watching a terrible movie playing out.

She lunged with startling quickness, an anaconda to its prey. She reached across his chest with one hand, grabbing the cell phone and tossing it onto the grass that surrounded the pool. She wrapped a powerful forearm tight around his neck and then used the other hand to clamp firmly over his mouth. In a violent motion, she yanked him backwards, off the inflatable raft and into the frightening cold of the water. He was startled, not yet realizing the reality of his situation. Beginning to understand his peril, he tried to use his hands to break free, but she kept pulling backwards and then sideways so he could not get his feet underneath him. He thrashed frantically with his legs, trying to find the bottom of the pool while tearing at her forearms with his fingernails. He dug into her flesh but in spite of the pain, her grip tightened, a vice grip, unyielding. She dragged him from the shallow end over the precipice of the deep end, using her strong kick to keep pulling him closer and closer to the deepest, darkest part of the pool. His fat body kept him afloat, and she had to double her efforts to hold his obscene head under the water line. She kicked powerfully, holding his head down, down, deeper into the hell where she wanted to send him. A piece of her mind wandered to all the days she and Ken and Hank and Mickey swam for hours on end, never touching the bank of the pond, diving and racing and holding their breath for what seemed like hours at a time before they finally hauled themselves out of the pond, still full of youthful energy. She came back to the reality of the place and time where she was and it did not cause her to falter, not at all.

A bolt of lightning ripped through the darkness, a sudden flash from the heavens. A simultaneous boom of thunder shook the earth forcefully enough to shake the water of the pool in the part not disturbed by the slow lessening of his kicks. Another flash, and another, and finally another, with their simultaneous thunderous booms, and then, finally, the storm moved off as quickly as it arrived. He kicked out once more, a futile, reflexive act when the mind and soul began to drift away, and his body became still, face below the water line, eyes protruding from his sockets, lifeless.

She held him that way for a while before she was convinced that his essence was fully and completely ended. She disengaged, aware of the harshness of her breathing and her total fatigue. A brief moment of panic set in as her strength faltered. She felt herself drop below the water line and begin to flail with her arms and kick frantically. She felt harsh water enter her lungs. She felt the overwhelming reflex to breathe, but she fought against it. She kicked once and then again, pulling hard with her hands and shoulders, fighting the cruelty of gravity as it pulled her down, cruelly attempting to end her life like she had ended his. With one last desperate effort, she kicked with all of her remaining strength and emerged from the depth of the deep end, saved from herself. She lunged for the edge of the pool, coughing up the same water he had swallowed moments before. She grabbed hold of the slippery tile and pulled her torso up and onto the concrete. She lay there on her stomach, lungs heaving, body drained of everything that mattered. She looked up and watched the violence of the storm move away in the distance, set to terrorize some other broken place.

She pulled herself out of the pool. She crawled onto the sod that he had planted around the concrete, holding herself up on her hands and knees. She leaned forward, folding her hands in the same way she had when she had prayed at the end of her bed not too long before. She stayed that way for a while until she finally pulled herself up and onto her feet. She looked back to the pool. His body was beginning to sink to the bottom. Left on the surface of the water was a pair of thick glasses and the elastic band that used to hold them to his head. The glasses sat in the water and stared upwards. She stared back, and for the briefest moment, imagined that his eyes continued to look at her through his thick, opaque lenses.

"Don't look at me like that. Now you're as free of him as the rest of us."

The glasses continued to look back at her until finally, they too began to sink, joining the lifeless thing that was now being pulled down by the inexorable suction of the filter at the bottom of the pool. Finally, the suction took hold, its unrelenting power holding him in place, entombing him at the bottom of his liquid grave.

She walked across the wet grass, calm now, soaked through her hoodie and sweats and running shoes. She moved silently around the edge of the house and retraced her steps down the driveway. She began to jog down the street, close to the woods to conceal her movements. When she got to Main Street, she quickened her pace. Some cars drove by. Even one car honked. The driver must have thought the chief needed a midnight run. Surely, she had been through a great deal and needed the solitude of a run and the solace of pushing herself to a physical limit, even if it was the dead of night after a sudden storm.

She ran on, past the downtown McDonalds and the old Tyre Rubber factory, long since dead. She ascended the hill, into the town center by the library and the civil war statue. She noticed that the base of it was still charred from when Hank's car exploded, the recent storm having no effect at cleaning away the remnants of the fire.

She ran past the town offices and the town diners and bars until she reached the road where she lived. As she drew closer, she found herself accelerating, sprinting now, arms pumping, knees churning, until finally, exhausted, she collapsed on her front yard. She crawled on her hands and knees until she pulled herself up and sat down heavily on the same rocking chair where she had placed Mickey Cumming's gun a few mornings earlier. She sat by herself late into the night until she finally stood up and walked into her house. She undressed quickly in the kitchen, using a dish towel to mop up the water that dripped from her clothes. She walked down into her basement, naked in the dark, and placed her wet clothes and running shoes into the drier. She turned and walked back up the stairs and then up to her bedroom. Her husband snored in bed. She put on some underwear, a t-shirt, and shorts and made her way quietly into her bed. She lay there, staring up at the ceiling, and surprisingly, fell asleep quickly. She slept peacefully, dreaming of pleasant fields, rolling hills, a wide river and new oak trees growing upwards toward a merciful sun.

Chapter 36

Eggs

Louise got up quickly the next morning. The storm from the night before had long since passed. The oppressive humidity that hung over Beaumont all summer had vanished and cool, crisp air cleansed the town, greeting the day with a spectacular blue sky.

She went to her basement to make sure her running clothes and shoes had dried. She returned them to her bedroom where she stored them back in the same place where she had found them the night before.

It was eight in the morning. The trip to Williamsport was scheduled to depart at nine from the town offices. She made herself coffee and sat at the kitchen table and waited for her husband to be roused by the aroma that drifted up to the bedroom. In a few minutes, she heard him stepping down the stairs. She stood up and poured him a mug. The two sat quietly. They sipped their coffee and waited for the sound of their daughters. After ten minutes, first Pammy and then Gretchen descended the stairs.

"Would you like some eggs?" Louise stood up and walked over to the refrigerator. She pulled out a carton of eggs before her daughters could answer.

"Yes, scrambled please," Gretchen responded.

"Me too," Pammy added.

"Can I have mine fried?"

"Yes, Hank, you can have your eggs fried," she smiled as she took out two separate frying pans. "Bacon?"

"Oh yes, please."

In a few moments, eggs and bacon were cooking on the stove and the girls were setting the table. Hank poured juice for the girls and Louise put the food on their plates. They ate quietly. The girls were glued to their cell phones while they munched on crisp bacon and perfectly cooked eggs with just a hint of cheese. The family stayed that way for another half hour until Louise' phone buzzed. She reached over to pick it up. It was Brad Timmons, Tommy's dad.

"We're over at the town offices, chief. Coach Monroe isn't here."

"Hmm. That's odd."

"We called him but he's not answering his phone. Do you think everything is ok?"

"I'm sure everything is fine, but I'll send one of my officers over to his house. He probably slept through his alarm."

"Well, the boys are waiting. They're so excited, you know."

"I can imagine."

She hung up her phone and placed it next to her breakfast plate.

"Who was that, chief?" Hank looked up from his eggs.

"Brad Timmons. Jack Monroe hasn't shown up for the trip

to Williamsport."

Hank looked at his wife. She pushed a button on her cell phone and speed dialed Betty.

"You better get over to Jack's house. He hasn't shown up for the big trip."

"I'm on my way, chief."

Betty hung up and Louise put the phone down once again. She took a bite from her bacon and finished her breakfast with her family.

"What happened to your arm, chief?" Hank instinctively reached for his wife's arm.

The girls looked up from their cells. She looked down.

"Hmm, I hadn't even noticed."

She took another bite of her eggs as a lovely sunshine brightened their kitchen.

Chapter 37

A Toast to a Friend

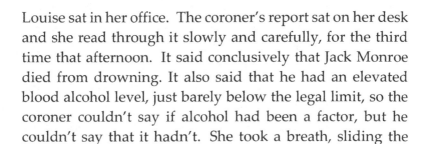

Louise sat in her office. The coroner's report sat on her desk and she read through it slowly and carefully, for the third time that afternoon. It said conclusively that Jack Monroe died from drowning. It also said that he had an elevated blood alcohol level, just barely below the legal limit, so the coroner couldn't say if alcohol had been a factor, but he couldn't say that it hadn't. She took a breath, sliding the report into a plain manila folder. She stood up and walked out of her office. Betty was at her desk.

"Can you please file this away for me?"

"Of course, chief."

Betty took the folder and stood up. She walked over to a cherry file cabinet against the wall that separated the police department from Mickey Cumming's former office. The window into his office had blinds that had been pulled down. The election of a new mayor was scheduled for a few months from then. Four or five people had tossed their hats into the ring. The town needed another mayor. Someone new would take Mickey's space and begin her or his own legacy.

Louise walked back into her office. She closed the door behind her. The glass window separating her office from the rest of the department had blinds of its own. She turned a handle that closed them, and the room became darker. It was late in the afternoon and the sun was beginning to set on the other side of the town offices. Louise sat in her chair. She reached down to the bottom drawer of her desk. She found a bottle of scotch hidden under some paperwork she had long ignored. She opened the bottle and looked at it before she took a long pull. She put the bottle back on her desk and let the warmth of the alcohol course through her veins. She reached over to the other side of her desk. She opened it up, reached in and pulled out a plastic bag. She opened it up and pulled out a pair of gold, kids Converse All-Star basketball shoes. She placed them on her desk and leaned back in her chair. She took another swig from the bottle of scotch. Her office was quiet except for the hum of air conditioning that kept her office tolerably cool. There was a knock on the door. It opened and Gallagher stuck his head inside.

"Too early for scotch, chief?"

"Perhaps."

"Mind if I sit down?"

"Do. Want some?"

She handed the bottle over to Gallagher. He looked at it for a moment before he took two, long swallows. He handed the bottle back. Louise used her sleeve to wipe the bottle before she took another drink. Gallagher looked over at the basketball shoes that sat on Louise' desk, then he turned back to look at the chief of police.

"Are you going to the funeral tomorrow, chief."

"I have to."

"I'll be skipping it."

"Do what you want, Gallagher."

She put her feet up on the desk. Gallagher looked at her and did the same. They sat that way as the chief's office darkened further. A final thin ray of light slid through the window, illuminating dust ghosts flitting about the room.

"Lots of dead people in your town, chief."

He reached over to take another drink of scotch. He shook the bottle. It was empty except for one tiny drop. He passed it back.

"Yes, too many."

"Maybe we should talk about Monroe's death."

Louise took the bottle of scotch. She reached over and dropped it into a wastebasket under her desk. She looked at Gallagher for a bit before she watched some of the dust ghosts begin to settle toward the floor of her office.

"I'm glad he's dead, Gallagher."

"So am I, chief. The bastard should have had his brains blown out and hung in the square. In a better world, we could have done that, once we knew the truth about the son of a bitch. In a better world, we could have done it with impunity, but that's not the world we live in, is it?"

He took his feet off her desk and sat straight in his chair. He looked hard at Louise. She looked back at him, holding his gaze without blinking.

"But it's curious, chief, that the man would die the day before his big trip to Williamstown."

"It is curious."

"Ironic that a man drowns in his own pool."

"That is ironic."

He folded his hands on Louise' desk. Her eyes danced in the gathering darkness. There was a knock on the door and Betty stepped in.

"Am I interrupting anything?"

"Come in, Betty."

She pulled up a chair and set three glasses down on the desk. Next to the glasses, she placed an unopened bottle of whiskey. She twisted off the bottle cap and poured the liquid into the three glasses. She handed one to Gallagher and one to Louise. She raised her glass and the chief and Gallagher joined her.

"To the mayor."

They held their glasses up and drained the whiskey.

"I found this when I cleaned out Mickey's office. Something tells me he wouldn't mind us toasting him."

"I'm sure he wouldn't, Betty."

Louise looked at the remnants of the golden liquid as it sat at the bottom of her glass.

"I was just telling the chief it was odd that Monroe should drown in his own pool, the day before his big trip," Gallagher said.

"That is rather strange." Betty took another drink. "I'm sure the kids are devastated, you know, with the big trip having to be cancelled."

"I'm sure they are," Louise murmured. "They're kids. There will be other trips. There will be other coaches."

Betty reached down and pulled something out of her back pocket. She leaned over and handed it to Louise.

"I found this at Jack's house, on the other side of the fence separating his pool from the rest of his backyard."

Betty placed an oversized cell phone on Louise' desk. It was cracked severely down the length of gorilla glass that was supposed to protect it from damage. It was a new model phone. The screen had been jarred in place, probably the moment it had been damaged.

"It's rather strange that an expensive phone like this would be so casually discarded," Betty said.

On the screen, Louise looked at a picture of a man standing over a little boy. She angled it so Gallagher could see it too.

"Hmm," he grunted as he leaned over to look at the image.

His face showed no emotion, like maybe he had seen terrible things like this before and this was just one other abomination that he would have to carry. The three of them sat there, drinking the rest of their whiskey. Betty turned to Louise.

"Can you talk to me some more about what's on Monroe's cell phone, chief?"

"It would seem like our hometown hero is, or was, a very bad man, Betty."

"Yes, it would seem so."

Betty looked over at Gallagher.

For the briefest moment, the thinnest of smiles formed on his face, only for it to disappear just as quickly. Betty looked back at her boss.

"Is there something I should know about that the two of you aren't sharing?"

She looked quickly between Louise and Gallagher. Their expressions remained flat, inscrutable, yet Betty couldn't help but notice a shared look of knowing between them, that they understood a truth that she could only hope to guess at, but that was dangled there, tantalizing in its horror and its simplicity. She smiled at both of them and reached over and filled their glasses. She raised her glass to her chief. Gallagher joined her and they threw back their drinks. They sat silently as the increasing darkness of the early evening settled heavily in the office.

Chapter 38

A Hole in the Earth

Jack Monroe's funeral was held later that week. It was a cold, rainy day, atypical of the hot, dog days of late August in Massachusetts. Where Ken Richardson and Mickey Cumming's funerals were packed, few people showed up for Monroe's farewell. There were a few members of the town council, their faces expressionless, sharing furtive glances. It seemed that none of the men that attended Jack's hometown hero celebration chose to attend his burial, the same boys he had coached over the years, sweet in their innocence when they had their lives ahead of them, pure in their hopes and dreams, devoid of fear at the time. They had stayed home and out of the rain, for reasons that they alone could admit to.

Some of Monroe's family members were there, but no one at the funeral could remember ever having met any of them before. Apparently, they hadn't shown their faces at any of Jack Monroe's championships. Whatever family had lived nearby had moved off years ago, leaving Monroe to his solitary pursuits.

Some of the boys on Tommy Timmon's baseball team, the same boys who were robbed of their trip to Williamsport when Monroe ended up dead at the bottom of his new pool, stood with their parents under lacking umbrellas. They wore their adorable Red Sox Little League uniforms, quickly getting soaked in the downpour. Tommy Timmons and his dad stood at the end of the row of boys. He clearly was the smallest member on the team. He fought to hold back the tears that burned in his hazel blue eyes. He had lost his beloved coach and it was difficult for such a little boy to lose someone so important. Role models are hard to find.

Louise stood under a tarp that hung over Monroe's grave. She was there simply because as chief of police, it was expected for her to attend, especially after his tragic and untimely death. So she did. She stood dutifully in the rain, a black trench coat buttoned high up to her neck. Someone asked her where Hank was. "Home," was all she said as the rain hardened.

The hole in the earth where Monroe would be dropped began to fill with fetid, oozing mud. Louise looked down and could see the ends of severed roots that had been sheared by an old backhoe that had done the job digging the pit earlier that day. The black soil stank and Louise had to pull back, fighting off the reflex to gag.

When it was finally all over, when all of the obligatory kind words were said by ignorant people, she walked away with the remaining mourners, turning her back to Monroe's pitiful grave.

No one was there when the town finally planted Jack Monroe into the ground. The rain was so hard that the canvas straps holding his coffin became slick. His coffin crashed into the mud, popping open slightly. The people working the backhoe didn't notice. They had other holes to dig. They covered the hole quickly, driving soaked, broken earth onto Monroe's fractured casket, like something awful might crawl out and walk among the townspeople sometime in a terrible future.

As Louise was getting in her cruiser, and the rain was hard and painful, and Jack Monroe was dead and gone, Tommy Timmons walked by with his father. The boy looked up at the chief of police of his perfect town. His angelic face was mired by long lines of tears that streamed down his unblemished cheeks.

"Chief, I don't understand. How come he had to die?"

Tommy's dad placed his arm around his son's shoulders while he held an umbrella to shield him from the cold rain. Louise stood and looked down at the boy. She had no umbrella so her hair was plastered against her skull. She looked around the parking lot and watched people walk away from the cemetery and climb into their comfortable cars, thankful to be finally out of the rain. She looked back to Tommy Timmons. She reached out and used her fingertips to clear the hair out of Tommy's eyes and touched her finger to his cheek, wiping away some of his tears.

"We can't always understand the why of things, Tommy."

She smiled at him as he and his dad walked away in the rain. She slid into her cruiser and drove off. There were other important matters that needed her attention at the police station.

If Tommy Timmons was lucky, the little league field would dry off tomorrow and he and his buddies would be playing baseball long into the heat of a brilliant, summer's day.

Rick Collins

ABOUT THE AUTHOR

Rick Collins is a retired teacher, a track and field, football and basketball coach, and an author who resides in Simsbury, CT. His first novel *It Emptied Us* was published in 2019 and is an exploration of friendships and triumph over tragedy as the characters come of age in a small town. His second novel *The Providence of Basketball*, explores race relations on the basketball court on the streets of Cranston, Rhode Island. A former athlete, Collins brings to his writing his experience of encounters throughout his career with racially and ethnically diverse athletes.

Collins resides in Simsbury with his wife Betsy and children.

A Run of a River

Made in United States
North Haven, CT
07 July 2023

38689458R00146